SAVE ME A SEAT

SAVE ME A SEAT

SARAH WEEKS AND GITA VARADARAJAN

SCHOLASTIC INC.

ISBN 978-0-545-84661-5

10 9 8 7 6 5 4   18 19 20 21 22

Printed in the U.S.A.   40

This edition first printing 2018

Book design by Mary Claire Cruz

FOR THE EXTRAORDINARY LUCY CALKINS,
WITHOUT WHOM THIS BOOK WOULD NEVER
HAVE HAPPENED.
—SW

IN MEMORY OF THATHA, MY BELOVED
GRANDFATHER, WHO TAUGHT ME HOW TO
TELL A GOOD STORY.
—GV

MONDAY:
CHICKEN FINGERS

CHAPTER ONE

RAVI

Most people in America cannot pronounce my name.

On the first day at my new school, my teacher, Mrs. Beam, is brave enough to try.

"Sur-yan-yay-nay," she says, her eyebrows twitching as she attempts to sound it out.

"*Sur-ee-ah-neh-RI-ya-nan*," I say slowly.

She tries again, but it is no better.

"I'm going to have to work on that," she says with a laugh.

I laugh too.

Suryanarayanan is my surname. My first name is Ravi. It's pronounced rah-VEE, with a soft *rah* and a strong *VEE*. In Sanskrit, it means "the sun." In America, people call me RAH-vee, with the stress on the first syllable. That doesn't mean anything.

"Patience is a virtue," Amma reminds me often.

She believes that, with time, people will learn how to say our names correctly. My grandmother tells her not to hold her breath.

We moved to Hamilton, New Jersey, a few months ago—May 13 to be exact. I am fresh off the boat, as they say. My father got a promotion at his IT company in Bangalore, so they transferred him to America. In India, Amma, Appa, and I had our own house with a cook and a big garden. We even had a driver to take us wherever we needed to go. My grandparents lived in their own flat nearby. Now we all live together in a town house, in a place called Hamilton Mews.

Things are very different here in America. Appa takes the train to work. We don't have a cook anymore, so Amma has to prepare all the meals herself. Our new house is much smaller than the old one. There is only one bathroom upstairs, which I share with my grandparents. I wouldn't mind so much except that Perippa likes to take long showers and Perimma leaves her teeth in a glass by the sink at night.

I learned to speak English when I was very young. We speak mostly English at home and I went to an English-medium school, but for some reason, people here in New Jersey have trouble understanding me when I speak. I am trying to learn how to swirl my tongue to sound more American.

My grandmother doesn't like it. "Be proud of who you are and remember where you come from," she tells me. "If you're not careful, you'll turn into one of *them*. Your grandfather didn't slave in the tea plantations so that his only grandson would become some rude, overweight, beef-eating cowboy."

I don't think Perimma likes America.

My school in India was called Vidya Mandir, which means "temple of knowledge." My new school is called Albert Einstein Elementary. Perimma could hardly wait to show off to all her friends at home that her grandson had been accepted to a school named after a scientific genius.

I'm not a scientific genius, but I am a very good student. My favorite subjects are math, English, and sports—especially cricket.

"Boys and girls, please welcome our new student,

RAH-vee," Mrs. Beam says after she has taken the roll call. "He's come to us all the way from India! Isn't that exciting?"

Mrs. Beam is short and round. When she smiles, her eyebrows touch each other.

As I look around the room, a sea of mostly white faces stares back at me. I feel a little nervous. It is my first day of fifth grade in room 506, and I am the only Indian in my class. There is one other, a boy named Dillon Samreen, but he doesn't count. He is an ABCD. *American-Born Confused Desi*. Desi is the Hindi word for Indian. I can tell Dillon is an ABCD, because he speaks and dresses more like an American than an Indian.

"Tell us something about yourself, RAH-vee," Mrs. Beam says, smiling at me.

"Yes, ma'am," I say, standing at attention.

Everyone laughs.

Mrs. Beam claps her hands. "Boys and girls, where are your manners?" she asks. "Go on, RAH-vee. We're listening."

I push up my glasses and continue. "My name is Ravi Suryanarayanan, and I just shifted from Bangalore."

Everyone laughs again. *What's so funny?* I wonder.

Mrs. Beam claps her hands. Her eyebrows are twitching like mad. "Boys and girls, is this how we welcome a new student to Albert Einstein?"

The room gets quiet. The spotlight is on me. I can feel the whole class staring. This is my first day of school in America, and things are not going well.

Mrs. Beam turns to me. "You can call me Mrs. Beam," she says softly. "And, RAH-vee? Here in America, students don't need to stand up when the teacher calls on them. Do you understand?"

Of course I do. I push up my glasses and rub my nose. It's something I do when I'm nervous.

Mrs. Beam comes over to my desk. She has a look of pity on her face.

"Don't worry, RAH-vee," she says, patting me on the shoulder. "You can introduce yourself to the class later, after you've had a little time to work on your English. We have a very nice teacher named Miss Frost in the resource room. I'm sure she can help you."

I want to say:

1. *My English is fine.*
2. *I don't need Miss Frost.*
3. *I was top of my class at Vidya Mandir.*

★ 7 ★

But here is what I do instead:

1. *Push up my glasses.*
2. *Rub my nose.*
3. *Sit down and fold my hands.*

My friends and teachers at Vidya Mandir would have a good laugh if they could see me now—their star student taken for an idiot. What a joke!

Mrs. Beam is writing out our homework on the board. I open my notebook and carefully copy down the assignment. Out of the corner of my eye, I see Dillon Samreen staring at me. He looks like a movie star straight out of Bollywood. His long, shiny black hair falls over one eye; with a quick jerk of his head, he shakes it away. Then he smiles and winks at me. I smile back. Dillon Samreen may be an ABCD, but I think he wants to be my friend.

CHAPTER TWO

JOE

My name is Joe, but that's not what most people call me. Not at Einstein anyway. I've never been a big fan of school—except for lunch. Eating is the one thing I'm really good at. I've always been tall for my age, but lately I've been growing so fast my clothes don't fit anymore, even the ones we bought a few weeks ago. I'm *always* hungry.

A lot of kids wouldn't be caught dead eating school lunch. They call it *mystery meat* and *slop*, but I don't mind. Every week it shows up in the same order: chicken fingers, hamburgers, chili, macaroni and cheese, pizza. By the way, it's not a coincidence that

Tuesday is burger day and Wednesday is chili day, because at Einstein, hamburgers get recycled. It's not as bad as it sounds. The leftover burgers from Tuesday get dumped into a big pot with beans and some other junk and, *presto chango*, on Wednesday you've got chili.

Everybody knows I don't talk much at school. My best friends, Evan and Ethan, used to call me Blabbermouth as a joke, but I guess I'm not going to be hearing that much now, since they both moved away over the summer. To be honest, they were a little weird, but I'm going to miss them anyway.

Evan, Ethan, and I ate lunch together every day last year, and they had to go to the resource room for extra help, same as me. (Not that we had the same problems—for one thing, they were both super hyper and I'm not.) This year, I'll have to go by myself to see Miss Frost, and I'm not sure who I'm going to eat lunch with. Probably no one.

People think you're unfriendly if you don't talk to them. But they don't understand that it's a problem for me that it's so noisy in the cafeteria.

My brain and noise don't get along.

Last year, I had Mr. Barnes for my teacher. Mr. Barnes is epic. He can bounce a Hacky Sack off his knee a hundred times without messing up. I had never even heard of a Hacky Sack until Mr. Barnes brought his to school. It was pink, which Dillon Samreen thought was hilarious. He said something mean about it behind Mr. Barnes's back, and all the girls laughed. Sometimes I wonder what's wrong with girls, but then I remember I already know what's wrong with girls—*everything*.

Mr. Barnes is African American. He shaves his head and wears bow ties—real ones you have to tie yourself. He must have talked to Miss Frost about me, because he never asked me to read out loud in front of the class or come up to the board to do math problems. He understood those things are hard for kids like me.

Some people don't mind having everybody looking at them—Dillon Samreen, for instance. He wears his pants pulled down low, with his underwear sticking out the top. He wants people to see it. His boxers have dollar signs on them, or dice, or lobsters, and he has special ones for holidays too, with candy corn or Christmas trees or red hearts for Valentine's Day. Dillon is famous for his boxers, but his real claim to fame is his tongue, which is long and pointy like a devil's. When he sticks it out, it makes the girls scream. He thinks he's the smartest kid at Einstein, and he might be right. He's definitely the meanest. Sometimes I wonder what it would be like to be Dillon Samreen, but that is something I'll never know.

Mr. Barnes was the first teacher I ever had who liked me. Miss Frost likes me, but she likes everybody, so it doesn't count. On my final report card, Mr. Barnes wrote that I was "a valuable member of the community." My mom was so proud she stuck it on the refrigerator with a magnet. It's still there.

TODAY IS THE first day of school, and Mr. Barnes is the first person I run into when I get here. He's wearing a red bow tie with little blue whales on it. I'm pretty sure it's new, or at least I've never seen it before. Last year, Mr. Barnes had seventeen different bow ties that he always wore in the same order—starting with the green one with white diamonds and ending with the orange-and-purple-striped one. Mr. Barnes's bow ties were another one of my favorite sequences.

"Yo, Joe," he says. "How's it feel to be a fifth grader?"

"Good," I tell him. "At least so far."

Maybe this year will be different, I think. *Maybe Dillon Samreen won't be in my class.*

But when I get to room 506, there he is, standing over by the windows with his underwear hanging out. Polka dots.

Lucy Mulligan and a bunch of her annoying girl friends are standing around him, chanting, "Do it, do it, do it!" They want him to stick out his tongue, but Dillon won't.

"Come on, Samreen, let's give 'em what they want!" Tom Dinkins shouts before sticking out his own tongue and wagging it at the girls.

Tom Dinkins is a Dillon Samreen wannabe. The girls don't care about his tongue.

"I warn you," Dillon tells his fan club, "I think it grew a little over the summer."

Lucy and her friends start jumping up and down, screaming, "Eeeew!"

One thing I will say about Dillon Samreen: He really knows how to play a crowd.

All the screaming starts to get to me, so I do the *in-two-three, out-two-three* breathing Miss Frost taught me. If that doesn't work, I'll have to use my earplugs. I always keep a pair in my pocket just in case. They come in different colors, but I like the tan ones best, because they don't show as much. They're made out of some kind of squishy foam rubber, and when I wear them, I can still hear people talking, only it's softer, like when you're underwater or have a pillow over your head. I'm allowed to wear my earplugs in school whenever I want, but mostly I use them in the cafeteria, on the playground, and in gym class.

"Settle down and take your seats," announces Mrs. Beam, my new teacher. This is her first year teaching at Einstein, and she looks a lot younger than any of the other teachers I've had. She's shaped kind of funny—wider on the bottom than the top—and she's shorter than me, which is weird, considering that she's my teacher. She seems nervous, and there's something freaky about her eyebrows.

At Einstein, kids have to sit in alphabetical order. Every year since kindergarten, my seat has been right behind Dillon's. I know the back of his head by heart. Mrs. Beam has made name cards for us and put them on the desks, but when I go to take my seat behind Dillon, somebody's already sitting in it. He's a shrimpy-looking kid with thick glasses and greased-down black hair parted on the side. I've never seen him before, and I'm not sure where he's from. His skin is darker than mine, but not as dark as

Dillon's or Caleb Burell's. When I look at the card sitting on his desk, I see his name is about a mile long and full of *y*'s and *a*'s.

He seems kind of nervous too. He keeps rubbing his nose and looking down at his hands, which are folded in his lap like he's in church or something. His shirt is so white it hurts my eyes to look at it, and he's got it tucked in and buttoned up all the way to the top. When Mrs. Beam asks him to tell the class about himself, he stands up like he's in the army and calls her ma'am—which is about the only word he says that you can actually understand. Everybody starts laughing, and for a minute, I think, *Hey, maybe fifth grade isn't going to be so bad after all.*

Maybe Dillon Samreen will decide to pick on this new kid with the weird name and the funny accent instead of me.

CHAPTER THREE

RAVI

Mrs. Beam tells us we are going to play some games called icebreakers. I can already tell that school in America is going to be easy for me. At Vidya Mandir, we never played games during class. On my first day of fourth grade, my teacher, Mrs. Arun, gave us a test! The first game Mrs. Beam teaches us is called Fruit Salad. I am on the team called Bananas, and Dillon is on the Apples. Another game is called Wink Murder. In this game, one person is the "murderer," and he or she has to knock people out by winking at them. I find this game a bit confusing because even when Dillon is not the one chosen to be the murderer, he still winks at me. The last game we play is called Venn Friends. For this game, Mrs. Beam assigns us partners. I hope that she will put me with Dillon Samreen, but instead my partner is a pale, skinny girl called Emily Mooney.

"You'll have a few minutes to interview each other," Mrs. Beam explains. "Find out as much as you can about your partner. For instance, what kind of music does he or she like? What is his or her favorite food or sport? When you've finished your interviews, you'll create a Venn diagram showing all the things you have in common."

"What the heck?" says a red-haired boy with freckles.

He doesn't know what a Venn diagram is, so Mrs. Beam has to explain it. At Vidya Mandir, we learned how to make Venn diagrams in third grade.

"Each of you must draw a circle and fill it with a list of things that your partner enjoys," Mrs. Beam says. "Then you and your partner will draw two overlapping circles. Where the circles intersect, you'll make a list of all the things you've discovered you have in common."

At first, I think this will be an easy game for me, but every time I try to ask Emily Mooney a question, she giggles and says, *"What?"* Then, when I try to answer her questions, she does the same thing. Appa says that someday I will be interested in girls, but that day has definitely not come yet. When Mrs. Beam calls time, the only thing Emily Mooney and I have found to place in the intersection of our diagram is that we are both in room 506—and that was my idea. I am glad when Mrs. Beam tells us it's time to get ready for lunch.

At Vidya Mandir, our lunch period began at one o'clock. Fifth graders at Albert Einstein Elementary School eat lunch at 11:30 in the morning. When I get to the lunchroom, the first thing I do is look for Dillon Samreen. In India, my best friend, Pramod, and I always ate lunch together. Afterwards, we'd play cricket in the field behind the school.

I spot Dillon standing in the queue waiting to buy his lunch. They are serving something I have never heard of before called chicken fingers. Most of the tables are filling up quickly, but I spot an empty table on the opposite side of the lunchroom and sit down. While I wait for Dillon to join me, I carefully lay out the cloth napkin that my mother packed for me, neatly folded with a spoon tucked into it. I'm not feeling very hungry, but Amma will be upset if I don't eat the lunch she made me.

"Uppuma made with pure desi ghee," she said as she stirred the pot this morning. "Semolina will give you plenty of energy for your first day of school, Ravi."

"Too lumpy," Perimma criticized, looking over my mother's shoulder as she cooked.

I am just getting ready to open my stainless steel tiffin box, when Dillon Samreen walks by carrying his tray. I caught a glimpse of his underwear earlier in class. There are red dots on it. I think about my own underwear, clean white Hanes from Kohl's that my mother insists on ironing. There's no way I would ever let my underwear hang out like that, whatever that kind of underwear is called.

I thought Dillon and I would eat lunch together today, but instead he goes and sits down at a table in the corner by the window with some of the other boys. I had been looking forward to having a good laugh with him about Mrs. Beam suggesting that I need special help. But it's okay. I'm not worried. I'm sure that Dillon and I are going to be friends. He's been smiling and winking at me all morning.

A big white kid with yellow hair and a wrinkled

shirt comes and puts his tray down at the other end of my table. He doesn't say hello to me, just sits down on the bench. He's so big the table shakes and my tiffin box jumps. I recognize him as the guy who sits behind me in class, but I don't remember his name.

He doesn't seem very friendly. He picks up his fork and starts shoving food into his mouth and doesn't stop eating until his plate is clean. I think maybe he forgot to eat breakfast. And what's that he's got in his ears?

I'm feeling a little hungry now too. I spread the napkin on my lap and bend down, sniffing at the uppuma. Perimma was wrong—it's perfect, not lumpy at all, so I gobble it down quickly. I need to wash my hands and rinse my mouth, but for some reason, there isn't any sink in the lunchroom. I look at my watch. I still have ten minutes left until the bell rings, so I tuck the spoon back into the napkin, place it in my tiffin box, and buckle the lid.

As I'm on my way out of the lunchroom to wash up in the boy's bathroom, a roar of laughter comes from the table in the corner by the window. Dillon Samreen must have made a good joke because every-one is slapping him on the back and treating him like he's a hero. I smile to myself. I know exactly how it feels to be that guy. I know something else too: Tomorrow I will not be eating my lunch alone. I will be sitting at the table in the corner by the window right next to Dillon Samreen.

CHAPTER FOUR

JOE

It's Monday, so the cafeteria is serving chicken fingers with canned peas and apple slices. I had a big breakfast and it's only 11:30, but I'm so hungry I could eat a horse. For real. I go through the line as fast as I can. Ethan and Evan and I used to eat at the round table near the milk machine, but things are different now. I have to lie low. After I pay for my food, I carry my tray over to the other side of the cafeteria, keeping my head down the whole time. So far, so good.

There's a long table against the back wall. Nobody ever sits there because it's near the trash cans. Fifth grade has the first lunch period, though, so I figure the smell won't be too bad yet. I sit down, put in my earplugs, and inhale everything on my plate in about three seconds. I'm still hungry, but I don't want to take any chances by going back for more. As I'm sucking down the last of my chocolate milk, I notice someone sitting all the way down at the other end of the table. It's that shrimpy new kid from my class—the one with the big glasses and the long name who sits in front of me. He's got this weird-looking lunch box open in front of him and he's eating something that looks like scrambled eggs.

Robert Princenthal walks by and accidentally bumps my shoulder. At least I think it's an accident. Robert is another Dillon Samreen wannabe. The difference between him and Tom Dinkins is that Robert isn't mean when he's on his own.

"Sorry about that, Puddy Tat," he says, and keeps going.

My name is Joe Sylvester, but thanks to Dillon Samreen, I am known at school as Puddy Tat. It's on account of that thing that Tweety Bird always says to Sylvester the cat in the old Looney Tunes cartoons. You know, *"I tawt I taw a puddy tat."* I wish people would call me Joe, but when Dillon Samreen decides he's going to call you something, whether you like it or not, that's what everyone else is going to call you too. So at school I am Puddy Tat, Puddy, or Pud for short.

"Giving a person a nickname is a way of saying you like them," my mother said when she found out about it.

"Trust me," I told her, "Dillon Samreen doesn't like me."

"What's not to like?" she'd asked, kissing the top of my head.

She always does stuff like that, which is why we had to have the "big talk" this morning.

"Pretend you don't even know me," I told her. "And promise you won't do any of your corny mom stuff."

"I promise," she said, then made an X over her heart with her finger.

We'll see, I thought.

The new kid is busy eating his lunch, and I'm done with mine, so I just sit there for a while watching Dillon Samreen. I do that a lot—not because I want to, but because I have to.

One time in second grade, when I put my jacket down on a bench out on the playground, Dillon filled the pockets with dirt. Another time he slipped one of those little packets of ketchup in my homework folder and pounded on it with his fist to make it pop. He's always grabbing the back of my shirt, or trying to punch or trip me when nobody's looking. His favorite thing of all is to sneak up behind me and make a loud noise because he knows how much that freaks me out.

It wasn't until last year that I realized Dillon was a klepto. His parents are loaded, so he doesn't need the stuff he steals. He just does it for fun. He'll take anything he can get his hands on—a pencil sharpener, a glove, a retainer case—it doesn't matter. Whatever it is, he shoves it down the front of his pants for safekeeping. Since I never take my eyes off him, I've seen him do this a million times. But I don't ever tell on him, because what good would it do? He'd just fast-talk his way out of it and find a way to pay me back double.

After my mom found the dirt in my pockets, she suspected something might be going on.

"Is that Samreen boy bothering you?" she asked.

"No, Mom," I lied.

"We can talk to Miss Frost about it," she suggested.

"No!" I shouted. "Everything's fine."

"I worry about you, Joey. You never have anyone over to the house."

"I have lots of friends at school," I told her.

"Like who?"

"Ethan and Evan."

"The Burdock twins?" she'd said. "Those boys are so wild."

She didn't know the half of it. Ethan once stole his father's car keys and drove around the neighborhood in his pajamas, and even though Evan never got caught, I knew for a fact that he was the Bathroom Bandit of Einstein—notorious for drawing dirty pictures on the bathroom walls and throwing wet toilet paper balls on the ceiling.

Dillon and his buddies are busy yukking it up, so I figure it's a good time for me to go empty my tray. I guess the new kid must have left when I wasn't looking, because he and his funny-looking lunch box are gone now. I pick up my tray and make it as far as the trash cans before my luck runs out.

"Hey, Pud." Dillon comes over to me and puts his arm around my shoulders. "How's it going?"

My heart starts pounding and I feel myself go wet under the arms. Dillon Samreen is like one of those crocodiles you see on the Discovery Channel, lurking underwater with just his eyes showing, waiting to grab anything dumb enough to come within his reach.

"I'm good," I say, trying to duck out from under his arm.

He tightens his grip on my left shoulder, and with his other hand pulls the earplug out of my right ear, drops it on the floor, and crushes it with his shoe like a bug.

In-two-three, out-two-three.

"Listen, Pud, before you go, can I ask you something?" he says.

"I guess so." I look down at my shoes. It feels weird having only one earplug in. Lopsided.

"Is it my imagination or does that new lunch monitor look familiar?"

Dillon puts his mouth so close to my ear it makes me squirm.

I don't say anything, just keep my eyes glued to my shoes and breathe. *In-two-three, out-two-three.* I notice one of my shoelaces has come untied.

"Take a look, Puddy," says Dillon, jerking his head back to shake the hair out of his eyes. "Tell me if you recognize her too."

I don't move.

"Oh. Was that question too hard for you, Pud? You need me to talk a little slower? Take . . . a . . . look."

I don't want to look, but what choice do I have? I lift my head. My mom is standing over near the milk machine. She's wearing a red-and-white-striped apron and she has a whistle around her neck. When she sees me looking at her, she smiles and blows me a kiss.

I honestly think I might be having a heart attack. This is *exactly* what I was afraid would happen. It's the whole reason we'd had *the big talk*.

My face feels like it's on fire.

"Come on, Pud," says Dillon. "You don't want to hurt her feelings, do you? Blow her a kiss back."

"What's going on, Dill?" asks Tom Dinkins. He and Robert and this weird kid, Jax, have come over to empty their trays.

"Pud is about to blow a kiss to his mommy, the lunch monitor. And then she's going to change his poopy diaper."

Tom laughs.

"What the heck?" says Jax.

"No kidding, Puddy, is that really your mom?" asks Robert.

The bell rings, making me jump. Suddenly everybody starts rushing around, cleaning up and getting ready to go back to class. Dillon grins and winks at me, then lets go of my shoulder and walks away. He's done with me for now, but I'm not stupid enough to think it's over. My knees are shaking, but I manage to dump my tray and get out of there as fast as I can.

The rest of the afternoon is a total waste of time. Mrs. Beam calls on me twice, even though my hand isn't up.

It's only the first day of school and fifth grade already sucks.

CHAPTER FIVE

RAVI

....

The questions begin as soon as I step out of bus number 7A.

"How was your first day at Albert Einstein Elementary School, Ravi?" my mother asks. "Did you make any new friends? Do you have homework? Was the bathroom clean?"

"How many other Indians are in your class?" asks Perimma.

Amma and Perimma have been waiting for me at the bus stop. I could see them stretching their necks to find me even before the doors had opened.

Amma takes my green backpack off my shoulder

and carries it as we begin to walk towards our town house. I would rather carry it myself, but she insists.

"My teacher's name is Mrs. Beam," I tell them. "Homework is just some reading. And the bathroom is fine."

"How many other Indians are in your class?" Perimma asks again.

"None," I say. I don't tell her about Dillon Samreen because I know how Perimma feels about ABCDs.

As we pass the big pond located in the middle of our community, Amma points to it. "Promise me you won't go near that water, Ravi."

"You might fall in and drown. And I've heard there are leeches," warns Perimma.

The wind is blowing their sarees. Amma holds on to hers with her right hand. Her left hand is still carrying my backpack.

"Did you eat your lunch?" she asks.

"Please, Amma, can we first get home? I will tell you everything," I say. "I promise."

"Why can't you tell us now?" asks Perimma. "Did you not like the uppuma, Ravi? Don't blame me— didn't I say it was too lumpy?" When Perimma wants to make a point, she goes on and on about it like the rotating end of an electric drill. Perippa has a trick for that. He wears hearing aids, and when Perimma gets going on one of her long rants, he waits until she's not looking, then he turns them off.

Amma puts down my backpack. I can't believe what is happening. Right there in the middle of the street, she is checking my tiffin box to prove to Perimma that I've eaten my lunch. A few kids walk by, looking at us curiously. I bend my head, embarrassed, and stare at the spot between my sneakers. My glasses slip down my nose, and I push them back up.

"It's empty," says Amma proudly, holding the box out for my grandmother to see.

Perimma sniffs. "How do you know he didn't throw the lunch away?"

Amma doesn't say anything, just shakes her head and puts the tiffin box back in my backpack.

She and Perimma got along much better when they didn't live in the same house.

I reach over and grab my backpack from Amma, then run as fast as I can towards number 83. When we first moved to Hamilton Mews, I had trouble telling which house was ours because they all looked the same, but now I can tell without even looking at the number.

"Wait, Ravi! The door is locked. Perippa is napping and Appa is at the office!" my mother shouts, running after me, keys waving.

I wait on the doorstep until she and Perimma catch up with me and open the door. As we enter the house, I close my eyes and breathe in. The air is filled with the smell of Amma's cooking. She has already prepared my evening tiffin, a plate of dosas and a cup of Ovaltine—the same thing I ate every day after school in India.

I give her a hug and whisper in her ear so Perimma won't hear. "The uppuma was delicious."

"Thank you, raja," she whispers back.

DINNER IS LATER than usual because Appa's train is delayed and he doesn't get home until almost eight o'clock. After each bite, Perimma complains about the food.

"The rasam is too runny, and it tastes like dishwater. Have you ever heard of spices, Roshni?"

Appa comes to my mother's defense. "Let her be," he tells Perimma. "Roshni is doing her best. She is not used to having to do all the cooking herself."

"And I am not used to having to eat her runny

rasam," Perimma snaps back at him. "Did you know poor Ravi had only lumpy uppuma for his lunch?"

I glance at my mother and quickly change the subject. "Most people at Albert Einstein Elementary School don't bring their lunches from home," I say. "They buy school lunch, which costs two dollars and fifty cents."

"Is it vegetarian?" asks Amma.

"I wouldn't take their word for it," Perimma interrupts before I can answer. "I hear their salad oil has lard in it."

I decide not to tell them about the chicken fingers.

CHAPTER SIX

JOE

....

Mom is parked at the curb, waiting in the car when school lets out. Her old parking sticker from Mercy Hospital is still stuck to the windshield. She used to be a nurse there, but she and a bunch of other nurses got laid off right before Christmas last year. After that, everything changed. None of the other hospitals around here were hiring nurses, so Mom had to go on unemployment and Dad took a job driving a truck route because it paid more than he was making at his old job at Walmart. At the end of August when Mom found out Einstein was looking for a new lunch monitor, she applied for the job without even asking me first.

"Hop in," she tells me now, leaning out the window.

"No," I answer, too mad to even look at her.

"I'm sorry, Joe," she says. "It was an accident. Force of habit. Would a slice of pizza help make up for it?"

I shake my head. She broke her promise big-time. A million slices of pizza isn't going to make up for that.

"Hop in," she says again.

"No," I tell her. "I'm walking home."

Walking helps me think. Not that I really want to think about all the crummy stuff that happened today. Is it possible to have a worse first day of school?

After my mom drives away, I hear someone calling my name.

"Joe!"

I turn around and see Mr. Barnes hurrying to catch up.

"I was hoping I might run into you," he says. "How did it go today?"

I feel something hard swell up in my throat, and

for a minute, I'm scared I might start crying. But I swallow a couple of times and the feeling goes away.

"It was okay, I guess," I tell him.

"How do you like Mrs. Beam?" he asks.

I shrug. "She's shorter than me," I say.

Mr. Barnes laughs and pulls a pack of sugarless gum out of his pocket. He offers me a piece, but I shake my head. Sugarless gum gives me a headache.

"How's our old friend Mr. Samreen doing this year?"

I think about the name Dillon called Mr. Barnes behind his back the day he brought his pink Hacky Sack to school. A word my mother would wash my mouth out with soap for saying.

"He's not my friend," I say. "And no offense, but I don't think he's your friend either."

"The world is full of Dillon Samreens, Joe," Mr. Barnes says, unwrapping a piece of gum and putting it in his mouth. "The trick is not to let them get to you."

I wonder if Mr. Barnes has ever seen the look on the face of a zebra who's just stepped into a crocodile's mouth.

"Thanks for the advice," I say.

"If you want, I can write it down for you," Mr. Barnes says, pulling a pen out of his pocket.

The hard thing swells up in my throat again. Mr. Barnes knows I have trouble remembering things unless they're written down.

"That's okay," I tell him. "And by the way, I like your new tie." I wonder if anyone in Mr. Barnes's class this year will memorize his ties the way I did.

Mr. Barnes looks at his watch. He says he's sorry he has to run to a faculty meeting, but that I should feel free to stop by his room anytime to chat.

"Hang in there, Joe," he tells me as he walks away.

My stomach grumbles. I haven't eaten anything since lunch. I think about my mother's offer to take me out for pizza, and get mad at her all over again. How could she do that, blow me a kiss right in front of everyone? What part of *no corny mom stuff* does she not understand?

Normally it takes me half an hour to walk home, but I'm not in any hurry today. Mia, my dog, is waiting for me at the door when I finally get there. She's so happy to see me she falls all over herself, wagging her tail and trying to lick my face.

"Cut it out, Mimi." I laugh, pushing her away. "Your breath smells like liver."

Mom has been waiting for me too. One of her cooking magazines is lying open on the couch next to her. I can tell she's been crying 'cause her nose is red.

"What took you so long, Joey?" she asks. "I was beginning to worry. Can we talk?"

"I don't want to talk," I say.

I go into the kitchen, grab a couple of oatmeal cookies out of the jar on the counter, and pour myself a big glass of milk. Mia follows me upstairs to my room. I take off my sweatshirt, toss it on the floor, and shut the door.

I'm starving, but I'd rather skip dinner than have to sit across the table from Mom after what she did.

CHAPTER SEVEN

RAVI

Later, after my evening shower, Appa comes upstairs to say good night.

"I didn't even have a chance to ask you how your first day of school was, Ravi. Is it true what Perimma says, that there are no other Indians in your class?"

I tell Appa the truth.

"There is one other, but he's an ABCD."

"What sort of fellow is he?" Appa asks.

"Funny," I say. "And popular."

"Tell him your IQ is 135 and that you were first batsman on your cricket team at Vidya Mandir. That should impress him well."

"I don't need to impress him," I say. "He already wants to be my friend."

"There's no harm in showing off a little. You were top of your class at Vidya Mandir—does your new friend know that?"

I don't tell Appa that it's Mrs. Beam, not Dillon, who needs convincing. If my parents find out that she suggested I need special help with my English, they will insist on coming to school to complain.

When Amma comes in next to say good night, she tells me, "I'm making vegetable biriyani in the morning for you to take for your lunch with cinnamon sticks and coconut milk, just the way you like it."

"Thank you, Amma," I tell her, slipping the post-card I received from Pramod a few weeks ago between the pages of *Bud, Not Buddy* to save my place. Mrs. Beam only assigned us the first chapter, but I am liking the story very much, so I've read up to chapter eight.

"Don't forget to say your prayers, raja," Amma reminds me. Then she kisses my forehead and turns out the light.

My first day of school in America is over, and

though it wasn't perfect, I did make a new friend. Not only that, thanks to Appa I have an idea for how to fix things with Mrs. Beam. She told us that in the morning we will be starting with math, and *that* is going to change everything.

CHAPTER EIGHT

JOE

....

At five o'clock, Mom comes upstairs to tell me that dinner is almost ready.

"I made a meat loaf," she says. "The recipe is from *Bon Appétit*, so it ought to be pretty good."

My mom is a great cook, and even though I don't want to eat dinner with her, I'm so hungry now I'm actually seeing stars. The phone rings and Mom goes to answer it. I hope it isn't Dad checking in from the road. The last thing I need is for him to get involved in this whole thing between Mom and me. He'd probably just say what he always says: *Man up, Joe.*

The whole house smells like meat loaf. I try to ignore it, but I don't have the willpower to pass it up. I pick up my fork and start eating my dinner as fast as humanly possible. If I make sure my mouth is always full, Mom can't expect me to say anything to her. As soon as my plate is clean, I head to my room to read *Bud, Not Buddy*. Mrs. Beam told us to read the first chapter, but it was only eight pages long, so I decided to keep going. I'm a pretty decent reader when I'm not distracted, plus the story is good. It's about this orphan kid named Bud Caldwell and there's something about the way he talks that cracks me up. Like, instead of saying *all of a sudden*, he says *woop, zoop, sloop*. I just love the way that sounds—*woop, zoop, sloop*.

When Mrs. Beam wrote the assignment on the whiteboard, Dillon turned around in his seat and made a joke, calling it *Pud, Not Puddy*. Mrs. Beam didn't hear it, but Lucy Mulligan did and she laughed so hard she almost fell out of her chair.

Mrs. Beam gave us another assignment too— some corny "personal collection project," whatever that is. She didn't write it on the whiteboard with the other homework. Instead she just told us about it, which means now I can't remember anything she said. I tried to take notes, but she was talking really fast and then they started mowing the grass under the windows, so the only thing I know is that the project is due on Friday. I wonder if Miss Frost forgot to talk to Mrs. Beam about me.

I hear my mom coming up the stairs, so I quickly stash the book under my pillow, roll over on my side, and close my eyes. She knocks a couple of times, then she opens the door a crack.

"Joe?" she whispers. "Honey, are you awake?"

Mia is curled up on the bed beside me, and when she sees my mom, she starts wagging her tail, thumping it against my leg like crazy. I lie there like a rock, but I guess Mom can tell I'm not really asleep.

"It won't happen again, Joey. No kisses. I promise."

When she told me she'd applied for the job, I told her I thought it was a terrible idea. But she needed the work, and Einstein needed a lunch monitor, so who cares if the only thing I actually used to like about school is ruined now? Nobody, that's who.

"You won't even know I'm there," she tells me.

"Yeah right," I say, then pull the pillow over my head.

TUESDAY:
HAMBURGERS

CHAPTER NINE

RAVI

....

I lay out my math notebook, which Amma and I have carefully covered with brown paper. The label in neat cursive says:

Ravi Suryanarayanan
Grade 5, Albert Einstein Elementary School
Mathematics

It is my mother's handwriting. We went to Staples together last week to buy all my school supplies, but she insisted on writing out the labels herself. Even

Perimma has to admit that Amma's handwriting is beautiful.

"Your book is the first thing your teacher will notice, Ravi," Amma told me as she carefully wrote my name on one of the smooth white labels. "First impressions matter."

Now, sitting at my desk, I run my hand over my math notebook and smile. In India, I was the winner of the Math Olympiad three years in a row. I know all my multiplication tables till twenty. Appa is right: There's nothing wrong with showing off a little. I am sure that after this morning Mrs. Beam will realize what kind of student I really am, and this silly business about Miss Frost and special help will be over.

I place my new pencil box next to the notebook. Amma made sure that every item on the school supplies list was bought. Three mechanical pencils, two erasers, a six-inch ruler, two highlighters, four ruled notebooks, and a pack of 3M Post-its.

I keep looking over at Mrs. Beam, but I don't think that she has noticed yet how well prepared I am. She's busy writing on the whiteboard. In India, we only had blackboards. I loved the soft scraping noise the chalk made and the smell of the dusty erasers.

The desk in front of me is empty. I wonder if Dillon Samreen will be absent today, but at the last minute, he comes rushing into class and takes his seat. I'm glad my new friend is going to be here to witness what's about to happen. I'm sure he will be impressed.

"Let's do a quick review," Mrs. Beam announces.

Easy peasy! I think when I see the math problems Mrs. Beam has written on the board. Is this what fifth graders in America are doing? I was expecting something much harder, like maybe order of operations or something to do with decimals and fractions.

The big guy who sits behind me is groaning and moaning. I turn around to see what's wrong with him and notice his name card for the first time. *Joe Sylvester.*

As I'm reading his name, Joe Sylvester suddenly looks up. I smile, but he doesn't smile back. I can't believe kids in America are allowed to come to school looking like him. In India, we had to wear uniforms with dress pants, a collared shirt, and a tie. Joe Sylvester has on tracksuit pants and an unironed T-shirt. I face front again and straighten my back. Good posture is also on Amma's list of ways to make a good first impression. Joe Sylvester is slouching in his chair.

"Who would like to come up and show us how to solve the first problem?" Mrs. Beam asks the class.

I push up my glasses, take a deep breath, and raise my hand.

CHAPTER TEN

JOE

....

Please don't call on me please don't call on me please don't call on me, I think.

But I can feel Mrs. Beam's head turning my way. I groan. I have a feeling I know where this is heading. I sure hope Miss Frost remembered to tell Mrs. Beam about my APD.

Nobody knew anything was wrong with me until I started school. The first week of kindergarten, I spent most of my time hiding in the coat closet with my hands over my ears. My teacher, Ms. Kain, thought I was homesick, but that wasn't it at all. I didn't want to go home—I just couldn't handle the noise.

It turns out I have something called APD, which stands for Auditory Processing Disorder and means I have trouble listening. I'm not deaf—I can hear just fine. In fact, in a way the problem is that my hearing is *too* good. Which is why I go to Miss Frost. She gives me exercises to help my ears and my brain agree about what to listen to and what to tune out. She also has M&M's in her office—peanut ones—and she lets me eat as many as I want.

Miss Frost understands what's going on. But pretty much nobody else does. They don't understand how hard it is for me to follow directions when the electric pencil sharpener is going, or the door keeps slamming, or I'm worrying about whether someone is about to sneak up behind me and do something mean.

They also don't understand how much I hate to be put on the spot. Like when a teacher calls on me.

As Mrs. Beam turns my way, I slide down in my seat. Even if she knows about my APD, it doesn't mean I'm safe. Sometimes teachers think they're doing you a favor by treating you like you're no different from anyone else. The thing is, I *am* different.

I slide down even farther in my seat, as low as I can go without falling out. All I care about is not getting called on. It's not that I can't do math—actually, I'm pretty good at it. But standing up in front of the class makes me nervous, and when I get nervous, I forget what I'm doing and make mistakes.

It turns out today is my lucky day, though, because the new kid shoots his hand straight up in the air like an arrow. He's wearing another white polo shirt, buttoned all the way up. Even the sleeves have been ironed flat. They're stiff, and stick out funny, like little wings. His desk is covered with a bunch of junk, including some shiny new mechanical pencils, which Dillon keeps eyeballing with a klepto gleam.

Mrs. Beam looks right at me—at least I think she's looking at me, but then she calls on the new kid instead.

That was close.

CHAPTER ELEVEN

RAVI

....

"RAH-vee?" asks Mrs. Beam. "Would you like to come up to the board?"

This is it. The moment I've been waiting for.

"Yes, ma'am . . . uh, Mrs. Beam," I say quickly, correcting myself. In my hurry to get up, my knee bangs against my desk, and all my school supplies fall to the floor. I don't want to miss my chance to show off my math skills, so I quickly bend down to pick up my things. My glasses start to slip down my nose, but before I can push them up—ahhh! Something hard hits my forehead.

It's Joe Sylvester's head. Why has he done this,

bumped me with his rock-hard head? Can't he see I am trying to collect my stuff? I rub my forehead as he rubs his. His giant foot is stepping on my name card.

"Big Foot," I mutter under my breath.

Dillon hears me and laughs.

"That's rich," he says.

Big Foot just sits there like a lump, but Dillon gets right down on the floor beside me and helps pick up the rest of my things.

I thank him for his help, then take a deep breath and straighten my back. I am not going to allow anything to spoil this moment. This is my time to shine. I march up to the front of the class, take the blue marker from Mrs. Beam's hand, and face the whiteboard.

I look at the first problem, *23 x 13*. I close my eyes and the answer comes to me in a flash. *299*. But I am not going to blurt it out and take a bow. I am going to show Mrs. Beam something she has never seen before.

"What you are about to witness is pure magic, a secret handed down from ancient times," I say with confidence. There is complete silence in the classroom. I think Mrs. Beam's jaw has just dropped.

Take your time! I warn myself.

I write the two numbers, one below the other, in blue marker. Then, with a red marker, I draw an arrow connecting the last digits of both the numbers. "Three times three is nine," I say aloud, writing 9 in the ones place with the blue marker. Then I pick up a green marker and draw two arrows like a cross. "Two times three plus three times one is nine." I use blue again to write 9 in the tens place.

I look at the class. No one is moving. My plan is working perfectly! I draw an orange arrow connecting the tens digits of both the numbers and then pick up the blue marker again to write 2 in the hundreds place.

"The answer is two hundred and ninety-nine!" I proclaim, underlining the answer three times in purple, then replacing the cap on the marker with a satisfying click.

Everyone is staring shell-shocked at the board, amazed by what I have just done. Dillon Samreen grins and winks at me. I think he is impressed. If this performance has not impressed Mrs. Beam as well, nothing will.

"RAH-vee," she says very slowly, looking at all the

arrows on the board, "your answer is correct, and your method is very colorful. But . . ."

But? What can she mean, *but?*

". . . we do things a little differently here," she goes on, giving me that pity look again. "Next time, we don't need to see the arrows—just the numbers will do."

The purple marker slips from my hand, falling to the floor. First my manners are too Indian for her, and now my math?

What will the next humiliation be? I wonder as I walk back to my desk.

As if in answer to my question, I suddenly feel my feet go out from under me. I have tripped over something, and when I fall, my glasses go skidding across the floor.

"What's the matter with you, Pud?" Dillon calls out. "Why did you trip the new kid like that?"

What have I done to deserve this? I haven't said a word to Big Foot (or Joe or Pudding or whatever his name is). First he bumps my head, and now he trips me with his giant foot?

"Oh my goodness, are you hurt, RAH-vee?" Mrs. Beam asks, rushing over to where I'm lying on the floor.

I want to:

1. *Show Joe Sylvester what I think of him and his giant foot.*
2. *Tell Mrs. Beam the only thing that is hurting is my pride.*
3. *Shout at the top of my voice—MY NAME IS NOT RAH-VEE!*

But here is what I do instead:

1. *Bite my tongue.*
2. *Pick myself up.*
3. *Go and get my glasses.*

Appa's advice has gotten me nowhere. I am right back where I started.

The only difference is that now, thanks to Big Foot, I have a bump on my forehead and a huge shoe print on my name card.

CHAPTER TWELVE

JOE

....

When Mrs. Beam calls on the new kid to come up to the board to do the first problem, he jumps out of his seat like a jack-in-the-box on a spring. His glasses slide down his nose and all the stuff on his desk goes flying, including his name card, which lands on the floor beside my desk.

R-A-V-I. Mrs. Beam has been calling him RAH-vee, but when he introduced himself earlier, I'm pretty sure he said his name was rah-VEE, with the accent on the second syllable. As I reach down to pick up the card, he reaches for it at the same time and we bump heads. *Ouch!*

Dillon gets down on the floor to help Ravi pick up his stuff. But I know what he's really up to. Quick as a flash, he puts one of those mechanical pencils down the front of his pants.

When Ravi finally makes it to the front of the class to solve the problem, he draws a bunch of crazy-looking arrows on the board, each in a different color. I think it looks cool, but Mrs. Beam isn't impressed. He seems pretty bummed out after that. I don't see what the difference is as long as he gets the right answer.

Then, as if things weren't bad enough, Dillon sticks his foot out and trips him. That's a Dillon Samreen specialty, kicking a person when they're already down. He tries to pin it on me, but anyone with half a brain would see through that. How could I trip him from ten feet away? My legs are long, but they're not *that* long.

While Ravi goes to get his glasses and Mrs. Beam tries to decide whether she needs to call the school nurse, Dillon reaches back and swipes another one of Ravi's mechanical pencils.

I feel bad for Ravi. I could definitely give him some pointers—like for instance, not to leave his stuff lying around, and to watch out for the winking. Dillon always winks when he's up to no good. Maybe at lunch Ravi and I will sit at the same table again. I wouldn't mind. His clothes are flat and his lunch box is weird, but other than that he seems okay.

CHAPTER THIRTEEN

RAVI

....

After my failure to impress Mrs. Beam with my Vedic math, and then the tripping episode, I can hardly wait for the morning to be over. At lunch, I will sit with Dillon Samreen and the other boys and come up with a plan for how to put Big Foot in his place. One time at Vidya Mandir, a boy named Hassan stole a pair of leather batting gloves from my sports bag. My friends and I caught up with him after school and pushed him into a corner until he cried like a baby and gave back the gloves.

"Please take out your social studies textbooks and open them to page ten," Mrs. Beam tells us. "Who would like to read the first paragraph to the class?"

Dillon starts waving his hand in the air, but Mrs. Beam chooses a boy called Keith Campbell instead.

"*Most Native Americans were forced to leave New Jersey during the seventeen hundreds,*" Keith reads. "*Descendants of New Jersey Native American people hid or . . .*"

He stops before the next word.

"The word is *assimilated,*" says Mrs. Beam. "Class, please repeat after me."

We all say it together. *Assimilated.*

"Can anyone tell me what that word means?" Mrs. Beam asks.

Mine is the only hand that goes up.

"Yes, RAH-vee?" says Mrs. Beam.

I start to stand up, but catch myself in time. I have been awarded another chance to impress Mrs. Beam, and I am not going to give her any reason to find fault with me.

"Assimilate: to consume and incorporate

nutrients into the body after digestion," I say confidently.

Mrs. Beam smiles, but she has that pity look again. "I'm sorry, RAH-vee," she says, "I'm afraid I couldn't understand you. Because of your accent, you're going to need to speak more slowly in class if you want to be understood."

My face burns. Is there nothing I can do right? But I refuse to give up. I swallow my pride and try again.

"*Assimilate,*" I say, slowly swirling my tongue around the words to make them sound more American. "*To consume and incorporate nutrients into the body after digestion.*"

"Thank you, RAH-vee," Mrs. Beam says, but the pity look is still there. "In this context, however, the word *assimilate* means to try to fit in. Don't feel bad, it was a very good guess."

A *guess*? Is that what she thinks? My answer was correct. I am 100 percent certain of that. I have a photographic memory. I can still see the definition from my fourth-grade science notebook clearly in my mind.

Mrs. Beam asks Keith Campbell to continue with his reading.

"*Descendants of New Jersey Native American people hid or assimilated into white society.*"

"Very good, Keith," Mrs. Beam says when he has finished reading, then she looks around the room. "Who would like to read the next paragraph? How about you, Joe?"

Big Foot practically falls out of his chair. "No way," he blurts.

"*Excuse me?*" says Mrs. Beam.

Her eyebrows are twitching like electrified caterpillars. Mrs. Arun would never have allowed a student to speak to her that way. I wonder what Big Foot's punishment will be. But just then the door opens and a woman with white hair like a mop sticks her head inside.

"I'm here for Joe," she says. "I'll keep him for the rest of the afternoon if that's all right."

"That will be fine," says Mrs. Beam. "Oh, and did you get my note about our new student? I think he could use a little help."

Could this mop top be Miss Frost? I wonder.

"I did get your message. If you want, I can take him right now," says Mop Top. "The two of us can get acquainted, and if it seems like a formal assessment is in order, we can deal with the paper-work later."

What is she talking about?

"RAH-vee," says Mrs. Beam, "go with Miss Frost and Joe, please."

I look up at the clock. 11:25.

"What about lunch?" I ask.

"You can eat with Joe and me," says Miss Frost. "Do you buy school lunch or bring it from home?"

"From home," I say softly.

I don't want to eat my lunch in the resource room with Mop Top and Big Foot. I want to go to the lunchroom with my friend.

"RAH-vee," says Mrs. Beam. "Miss Frost is here to help you. Please take your things and go with her. Hurry up now."

I want to:

1. *Tell her I don't need help.*
2. *Show her that she is the one who doesn't know the meaning of assimilation.*
3. *Insult her hairy caterpillar eyebrows.*

But here is what I do instead:

1. *Sigh loudly.*
2. *Put my things in my backpack.*
3. *Go and get my tiffin box.*

CHAPTER FOURTEEN

JOE

....

Talk about perfect timing! I could kiss Miss Frost.
Well, not really. But I am happy to see her.

"I'll keep Joe for the rest of the day," she says.

Fine by me.

Mrs. Beam asks Miss Frost to bring Ravi along
too. He seems kind of mad about it. I was mad too
when I first started going to see Miss Frost. I didn't
like the way kids looked at me when she came to
get me out of class. Now I'm used to it. I like Miss
Frost, and I like being in the resource room partly
because it's quiet there, and partly because of the
M&M's—peanut M&M's come in red, green, yellow,

brown, orange, and blue, and they all taste exactly the same.

I walk down the hall next to Miss Frost. Ravi walks a few feet behind us and doesn't say a word.

"Here we are, RAH-vee," says Miss Frost when we get to her room.

Miss Frost's voice sounds like a cartoon bird—chirpy and high. Her hair reminds me of those long strips of cloth they drag over your car when you go through the car wash. She holds the door open for us, but Ravi just stands there.

"Is something wrong, RAH-vee?" Miss Frost asks.

Ravi pushes up his glasses and rubs his nose, then he puts his shoulders back and stands up really straight.

"My name is not RAH-vee," he says. "It's pronounced rah-VEE. I'm not going to bother to tell you how to pronounce my surname, because you'll never be able to say it right."

Miss Frost looks surprised.

"I'm very sorry if I mispronounced your name," she says. "I certainly didn't mean to offend you."

"I don't belong here," he says, pushing his glasses up again. "I speak perfect English. I was at the top of my class in India. My IQ is 135. I don't need special help. I'm not like *him*."

He points his finger at me.

I'VE BEEN COMING to Miss Frost's room since kindergarten. She was the one who figured out I have APD. My mom cried when she heard. My dad just got mad. He thinks APD is made up. He says doctors do that all the time to make money.

"Have a seat, Joe, and I'll be right with you," Miss Frost tells me now.

I sit down, dig a blue peanut M&M out of the big bowl in the middle of the table, and start sucking on it.

Rah-VEE. Rah-VEE. I say it to myself a few times until it starts to feel natural. I bet I could learn how to say his last name too if I wanted to, but why should I bother? I have more important things to think about. Like the fact that my dad called to say he's cutting his trip short and coming home early. I have a feeling it's because my mom told him about what happened in the cafeteria yesterday.

Miss Frost takes Ravi over to the other side of the room to the listening lab. He sits down and puts on a pair of headphones, but his legs are jiggling around under the table and I can tell he's still mad. For a minute, I thought maybe we could be friends, but now I know that's not ever going to happen.

Whatever.

After Miss Frost gets Ravi set up in the listening lab, she comes over and sits down beside me.

"Are you okay, Joe?" she asks.

I shrug and dig another blue peanut M&M out of the bowl. Blues are my favorite.

"Ravi was upset," she says. "He's a long way from home and still adjusting. I'm sure he didn't mean to hurt your feelings."

"He didn't," I tell her. "Everybody thinks I'm dumb. I'm used to it."

Miss Frost looks sad.

"Did you know your mom stopped by to see me on her way to work this morning, Joe?" she asks.

I shake my head. Why can't my mother keep her nose out of my business?

"Can we talk about something else, please?" I say.

"Like what?" asks Miss Frost.

I try to think of something that has nothing to do with my mom or her new job. "Did you know that if you suck on a peanut M&M long enough and you're careful not to bite down, you can actually feel each one of the layers dissolving in your mouth?"

Miss Frost smiles.

"Go on," she tells me.

"Most people probably think there are only three layers in a peanut M&M, but it's not true—there are four. The first one is the hard colored part on the outside; next there's a thin white layer—that's the part most people don't know about. Then comes the chocolate, and when that's gone, if you've done it right, you end up with a nice smooth peanut sitting on the end of your tongue."

Miss Frost is still smiling. "That's a very interesting observation, Joe," she says. "It's also a sequence."

Sequences are something Miss Frost and I have worked on a lot together. She says if I can think about things in order—*first, next, then,* and *finally*—it will help my brain stay organized.

"Pick your distractors," Miss Frost tells me.

I get up and go over to a shelf filled with things like kitchen timers, windup toys, and music boxes. I choose an old Mickey Mouse alarm clock and a battery-operated snow globe with a Santa Claus wearing a Hawaiian shirt inside. As I carry them back to the table, I catch a whiff of something spicy. It must be Ravi's lunch.

"Ready?" Miss Frost asks me.

The alarm clock is ticking loudly. I set the snow globe on the table beside it and turn it on. A blizzard of glittering white snowflakes swirls around the plastic Santa Claus.

"Ready," I say.

She hands me a copy of *Sports Illustrated*.

"*First* find a page with no pictures on it, *next* circle all the words that begin with the letter *t*," she tells me. "*Then* copy the *t* words out on a piece of paper, and *finally* fold the paper in half and bring it to me. Got it?"

Tick, tick, tick. I tell my brain to ignore the sound of the clock and the swirling flakes in the snow globe and focus on what Miss Frost just said.

"Find a page with no pictures. Circle the words that begin with *t*," I say, repeating the instructions.

"Then what?" she asks.

The Santa in the snow globe is holding a sign that says, HOLLYWOOD, HERE I COME! That gets me thinking about Evan and Ethan. I wonder how they're doing in California. That gets me thinking about the part in *Bud, Not Buddy* where Bud tries to sneak onto a train with his best friend, Bugs, only he ends up getting left behind with some girl named Deza who wants to kiss him. I don't know what I'd do if some girl tried to kiss me. Probably bite her.

"Then what?" Miss Frost asks again.

Crud. I totally lost my train of thought. I hate when that happens.

"Um . . ."

"Focus, Joe," Miss Frost tells me.

Tick, tick, tick. I close my eyes, and try hard to remember the rest of the instructions she gave me a minute ago.

"Copy all the *t* words out and write them on a piece of paper, fold it in half, and give it to you."

"Way to go, Joe!" Miss Frost says, putting her hand up to give me a high five.

Miss Frost doesn't know that high fives are corny. I look over at Ravi to see if he's watching, but luckily he's busy looking at the dictionary. He asks again if he can go back to class, and this time Miss Frost goes over to talk to him. I can't hear what they're saying, but I guess she gives in and decides to let him go because he shoves his stuff in his backpack real fast and heads straight for the door.

Fine by me.

Miss Frost offers Ravi an M&M from the candy bowl, and even though there are plenty of other colors, wouldn't you know it? He reaches in and takes a blue one. What really ticks me off is that it's a double—two M&M's stuck together. Those are rare.

He doesn't say good-bye. He doesn't eat the M&M either, just puts it in his pocket and heads for the door. Something's different about him. He's not mad anymore; he seems more sad. Not that I care how he feels.

I'm glad he's leaving.

"Joe," says Miss Frost, "I'll be back in a minute. Then we can get lunch."

As soon as she's gone, I put down my pencil and dump the whole bowl of M&M's out on the table. I go through them one by one looking for doubles, but there aren't any more. Doubles are rare—especially blue ones. I'm kicking myself. How could I have missed that?

CHAPTER FIFTEEN

RAVI

....

The eyes are windows to the world, Amma always says.

When I was little, she would look into my eyes and tell me they were bright and sparkling, like my mind. That was before Dr. Batra discovered that I could hardly see. In kindergarten, I had a serious copying problem. I could never copy anything correctly from the board. While reading a book, I had to stick my face so close to the page that my teacher, Ms. Venkat, suspected that I had some serious reading issues. When she called my mother in to tell her to get me assessed, Amma had cried. She couldn't stand that they were questioning my intelligence. It was Dr. Batra who figured out that the problem was with my eyesight. Now I wear glasses. The power of my lenses is thirteen, and I can see the world clearly.

Miss Frost gives me a book called *Fun with Phonics* and tells me to read along with a recording of the first story. There is a picture of letters dressed up in funny clothes on the cover. This is ridiculous. Does she think I'm a baby? I pretend to be listening to the story, but instead I turn down the volume and shift the headphones away from my ears so that I can hear what Miss Frost and Big Foot are saying. He is talking to her about candy.

I hear footsteps and people laughing out in the corridor. I recognize Dillon's voice.

"Last one in line gets a wedgie!" he shouts.

Why must I be stuck in here listening to baby stories when I could be racing off to eat lunch with my new friend, Dillon Samreen?

I pull off the headphones and stand up. "I've listened to the story, ma'am. Please can I go now?" I ask, but Miss Frost tells me to sit down and eat my lunch.

Will I be trapped here forever like Bud Caldwell

was trapped in the shed with the angry bees? I open my tiffin box and slowly unfold my napkin. How sad Amma would be if she could see me now. No wonder Big Foot made such a fuss when Mrs. Beam called on him earlier to read aloud; he probably doesn't know how to read a word.

I notice the fat red book sitting on a shelf nearby and realize what I must do. I finish my vegetable biriyani in a few quick bites. Miss Frost is still busy with Big Foot, so she doesn't notice me get up and pull the heavy dictionary down from the shelf. I lay it on the table, open it up to the section marked *A*, then run my finger down the page. *Askew . . . assess . . .* Yes! There it is: *assimilate.* I narrow my eyes and slowly read out the words. *To take in, digest, incorporate.* Ha!

"I knew it, I knew, I knew it," I whisper, smiling to myself, and shaking my head from side to side. I will show Mrs. Beam this page, and she will have no choice but to admit defeat. I'll announce her mistake in front of the whole class, pump my fist, and take a bow.

How sweet my victory will taste!

In the meantime, I eavesdrop and find that Big

Foot is talking on and on about candy. He never says a word in class, but here he can't stop talking about chocolate and peanuts. Will it never end?

I look at the dictionary one last time, just to be doubly sure, running my finger along under the words, this time very, very slowly. I want to make sure I have not missed anything. *Take in, digest, incorporate* . . . I bend my head closer. There is something else.

To integrate, to fit in. My finger freezes. Can my eyes be fooling me? No. Thanks to Dr. Batra, I can see perfectly well. I read it again: *to integrate, to fit in.* I close the dictionary and quickly pull my social studies book out of my backpack, turning to chapter one. *In this context,* Mrs. Beam had said. I read the passage and my heart feels heavy. Consuming and incorporating nutrients has nothing to do with Native Americans in New Jersey in the 1700s.

Just a minute ago, I had wanted to:

1. *Announce my victory.*
2. *Pump my fist.*
3. *Take a bow.*

But instead this is how I feel:

1. *Embarrassed*
2. *Ashamed*
3. *Defeated*

Miss Frost comes and sits down next to me.

"I'm sorry to keep you waiting," she says. "I know that you're eager to get back to class, but I thought it might be a good idea for us to have a little chat."

What is there to talk about? The taste of victory is gone.

All I want is to dig a deep hole and hide my head in it forever.

"I'm here to help you in any way I can," says Miss Frost. "We have lots of ESL materials here in the resource room."

"ESL?" I say.

"English as a second language," she explains. "Mrs. Beam mentioned that she and some of the children have been having difficulty understanding you because of your accent."

I hang my head. English is not my *second* language—it is my *first*. My English is much better than my Tamil. Mop Top doesn't even know me, and now she is criticizing the way I speak?

"I can only imagine how difficult this must be for you," she tells me. "A new school, in a new country. Maybe it would help to speak with Mr. Garfinkle, our guidance counselor. He's very easy to talk to."

I feel like I am suffocating. Now I'm in need of some kind of counseling too?

"Please," I whisper. "Can I just go back to my classroom?"

"Of course," she says, and pats my hand. "Mrs. Beam should be back in her classroom by now. I'm sure she won't mind if you sit quietly and read until the others come back from lunch."

I nod my head, grateful that my torture is finally coming to an end. Then I quickly stuff my tiffin box and social studies book back in my backpack before Miss Frost can change her mind about letting me go.

Big Foot is looking at a magazine and doesn't even look up as I walk past.

"Would you like an M&M for the road?" Miss Frost asks me, holding out a big bowl full of colored candies. Amma doesn't like me to eat sweets, but I don't want to be rude, so I take a candy—a blue one—and put it in my pocket as I prepare myself for the long walk back.

Miss Frost and I walk down the corridor together. When we reach room 506, she turns to me. "How about we meet again next week?" she says. "Once you've had a bit more time to settle in." I reach to open the door, but Miss Frost puts her hand on my shoulder. "Before you go, can I tell you something? I think you've assumed something about Joe that isn't true. You and he could easily be friends."

I shake my head no. Why should I be his friend, after what he did to me?

"This morning in class he tripped me on purpose with his foot and nearly broke my glasses," I say.

"That doesn't sound like the Joe I know," says Miss Frost.

"Dillon saw him do it," I tell her. "He told me."

Miss Frost bites her lip, then says, "I wasn't there, but if he tripped you, he owes you an apology. And you owe him an apology as well, for implying that he might not be as smart as you are. Just because Joe needs help doesn't mean he isn't bright. You shouldn't assume things about a person before you know who they really are."

"People are making assumptions about me too," I

point out. "They think I can't speak English or do math. But that's not true."

Miss Frost nods her head.

"You see," she says. "Assumptions are often wrong."

She tells me to remember that.

CHAPTER SIXTEEN

JOE

....

When Miss Frost comes back to the resource room, she's carrying a tray with three hamburgers on it. One for her and two for me.

"Did anything happen in class this morning that I should know about, Joe?" she asks, tearing open a package of ketchup with her teeth and carefully squeezing a squiggly red line onto the top half of her bun. I'm already done with my first hamburger and about to start in on the second. I should have asked for three.

"I spazzed out a little when Mrs. Beam asked me to read," I say. "Did you tell her about my APD?"

Miss Frost nods.

I reach for a carton of chocolate milk and try to open the spout, but the paper keeps ripping. Miss Frost takes it from me and uses her fingernail to pull open the milk, then she hands it back.

"I was wondering if anything happened with RAH-vee in class this morning," she says.

"It's rah-VEE," I say. "And Dillon tripped him right after he did some crazy-looking math problem on the board. Is that what you mean?"

"He seems to think that you were the one who tripped him."

I shake my head.

"I guess maybe he's not as smart as he thinks he is," I say.

AFTER SCHOOL GETS out, my mom is sitting in the car waiting for me. We go through the same routine as the day before. She tries to convince me to let her give me a ride home and I tell her I'd rather walk. I walked to school in the morning too. I don't get mad that often, but when I do, I always stay mad for a while.

I have a couple of bucks in my pocket, so I stop at the mini-mart on the corner to buy a snack.

I had been planning to get a bagel and cream cheese, but instead I decide to buy a king-size bag of peanut M&M's.

Ever since I saw Ravi take that double blue one out of the bowl, it's been bugging me that I didn't find it first.

I pay for the M&M's and rip open the pack. Out of twenty-two, there are five blues, but no doubles. I eat them slowly, sucking off the layers, trying to make them last the whole way home. When I finally walk in the door, Mimi comes running. She rolls over on her back, and I give her a good belly scratch. Mom's out in the kitchen, and from the smell of things, I'm pretty sure she's making pork roast and scalloped potatoes. It's going to be hard to stay mad at her if she keeps this up.

"Joey," Mom calls. "Is that you?"

"Yeah," I call back.

She comes out of the kitchen, drying her hands on a dish towel.

"Hungry?" she asks.

My head tells me to go upstairs, but my stomach tells me where there's pork roast and scalloped potatoes, there might be apple crisp too.

"I'm starving," I say.

"Dinner won't be ready for another hour, but I just took a crisp out of the oven. You want some?"

Boy, do I. But between last night with the meat loaf and now this, I don't want her to think I'm a pushover.

"I'm still mad at you," I tell her.

"I know," she says.

I follow her out into the kitchen, where she dishes up a big bowl of warm apple crisp.

"Ice cream?" she asks.

I nod, and she puts a scoop of vanilla on top of the crisp. Perfect.

I take a bite and close my eyes, letting the taste explode in my mouth like fireworks.

"Are you ever going to forgive me?" she asks.

"Eventually," I tell her.

She gets busy washing lettuce. I'm glad she doesn't ask me about my day. I keep thinking about what Ravi said, and the way he pointed his finger at me. Even apple crisp can't take the edge off that.

"More?" asks Mom.

"No, thanks," I say, handing her the empty bowl. "I'm good."

WEDNESDAY:
CHILI

CHAPTER SEVENTEEN

RAVI

··

When Amma comes in to wake me, she has red chiles and salt in her hands.

"Sit still, Ravi," she says. "I'm going to take away the kan drishti, the curse of the evil eye."

Even though I haven't said a word to her about how badly things have been going for me at Albert Einstein Elementary School, somehow my mother has figured it out.

"The kan drishti is what's causing your problems, raja. I'm sure of it," she tells me.

I tried to hide my feelings yesterday when I returned home from school. Amma and Perimma picked me up at the bus stop, bombarding me with a million questions as usual.

"Did you show your Vedic math?"

"Was Mrs. Beam impressed?"

"Did she comment on how nice your notebooks look?"

"Did you enjoy the vegetable biriyani?"

"Leave me alone!" I begged them.

That was my mistake. For the rest of the afternoon, Amma and Perimma chased me around the house, offering me food and drink, hoping to pry some information out of me.

"What's wrong, Ravi?" Amma kept asking. "Has something happened?"

Perimma even threatened to email Mrs. Beam if I didn't tell her what was bothering me. There was no way I could tell them that I had been laughed at, disrespected, tripped, ridiculed, and forced to eat my lunch in the resource room with the very person who had tripped me. Amma would have been heartbroken. So I faked a stomachache and went to bed early.

Amma clutches the salt and chiles tightly with both her palms and slowly circles them around me three times clockwise, then runs downstairs and throws the potion on a hot skillet. There is a loud crackling sound and the smell of burnt chiles fills the air.

"I knew it!" I hear Perimma cry. "See how they crackle? Ay-yi-yo! Didn't I tell you things would be difficult for us in America? People are jealous. That's what it is. Jealous of our Ravi and his superior intelligence."

If only she knew what they really think of me at school.

I get dressed and go downstairs, where Amma has made two soft iddlies for my breakfast.

"Wait! First take this," says Perimma, shoving a spoonful of pink medicine into my mouth. It tastes horrible, but it is my own fault for having faked a stomachache.

"Everything is going to be okay, Ravi," Amma says. "I've baked some naan khatais."

My favorite cookies!

"The flavor is off," sniffs Perimma, tasting a crumb and wrinkling her nose. "You put in too much rosewater, Roshni."

Amma sighs. I can tell she is biting her tongue.

"You'll see, Ravi," she says as she carefully places the last crumbly round cookie in the box. "Mrs. Beam will be impressed."

"The naan khatais are for Mrs. Beam?" I ask, surprised.

"I know just how to win teachers over," Amma says confidently. "Offer the cookies to her first thing this morning. You'll see how things improve after that."

Appa comes in carrying his briefcase.

"Listen to your amma," he tells me. "Remember she has the black tongue."

Amma has a birthmark on her tongue. In India, a black spot on the tongue means you have magical powers. This may sound like a silly superstition, but believe me, when Amma says something is going to happen, it always does.

It's 6:58. The bus will be arriving in two minutes. Amma puts on her favorite blue sweater, picks up her saree pleats, hoists them just above her ankles, and tucks them in at her waist. Slipping her bare feet into a pair of rubber sandals, she rushes towards the door, but Appa stops her.

"Let him go by himself, Roshni," he says. "He's ten years old."

Perippa is sitting on the sofa dipping his biscuit in his morning tea. Perimma hands me my tiffin box and my jacket.

"Don't forget to tell Mrs. Beam the naan khatais are homemade!" my mother calls after me. "And remember to eat your lunch! I made a nice curry with okra and chickpeas, raita, and a flask of buttermilk too. Good for your digestion!"

TWO BOYS FROM my class are sitting in the front row of seats on the bus. One of them is Keith Campbell and the other is named Tim or Jim, I'm not sure which. They nod to me, and I nod back. I wish that Dillon Samreen rode on my bus. Pramod and I used to ride together and crack jokes the whole way to school.

I find a seat near the back of the bus and sit down, carefully balancing the box of cookies on my lap. All the way to school, I stare out of the window, wondering if my mother can be right. Will the kan drishti healing and the homemade naan khatais help to turn things around for me?

When we arrive at Albert Einstein Elementary School, I look up at the American flag flying on top of the silver pole. I think about my own flag with its blue spinning wheel at the center. Each of the twenty-four spokes represents a virtue. Mrs. Arun had a list of them written on her wall, and she made us memorize them in order. I think about number two on the list (courage), number thirteen (righteousness), and number fourteen (justice). *Be proud of who you are*, I hear Perimma's voice say in my head. *Remember where you come from.*

I take a deep breath, straighten my back, and step off the bus.

BIG FOOT IS standing near the door when I reach room 506. As I walk past him, I keep my eyes on his giant shoes. I will not allow him the pleasure of tripping me again.

When I present Mrs. Beam with the cookies, she smiles. In fact, she *beams*. Ha!

"How sweet!" she tells me.

Amma's black tongue was right. Thanks to the naan khatais, I have won over Mrs. Beam. Even her eyebrows seem friendlier today.

"We'll begin our morning with silent reading," she tells the class. "Following that, you'll go to gym."

Things are looking brighter for me already.

CHAPTER EIGHTEEN

JOE

....

When I was a little kid, if I fell down and skinned my knee, my mom would kiss it to make it better. I thought it was magic. But I'm not a little kid and I don't believe in magic anymore.

I decide to let my mom drive me to school, but we don't talk. At least I don't.

"Dad won't be getting in until late tonight," she tells me. "You won't see him till tomorrow morning."

I'm not in any hurry. Not that I don't miss my dad when he's on the road. I do. Sometimes we watch sports together and act like guys—burping and scratching and stuff. But it's been a while since we did that. Mom still hasn't said anything, but I'm positive I'm right about the reason he's coming home early. I know the drill. She's going to make us have a family meeting. I'll sit there saying nothing, my dad will tell me to "man up," and when it's finally over, nothing will have changed. Mom will still be the lunch monitor, Dillon Samreen will still be giving me a hard time about it, and fifth grade will still suck as much as it did before.

"Hey, Pud, Not Puddy," Dillon says as I walk into room 506. He's standing by the door, like he's been waiting for me. Lucy Mulligan giggles, which pretty much guarantees that the dumb joke will be following me around for a while.

The funny thing about Lucy is that she and I used to be friends. We went to the same nursery school when we were little, and sometimes after school we'd play together. She even had a sleepover at my house once when her mom and dad had to go out of town for a funeral. She wet the bed and cried. My mother put the dirty sheets in the washing machine, and Lucy made me promise that I wouldn't tell anybody at school about it. I never did.

Dillon is about to say something else, but then

his dark eyes slide to the left and there's that evil sparkle I know so well. I turn around to see what he's looking at. Ravi has just arrived with his green backpack and ironed blue jeans. For some reason, he's looking especially shrimpy today. His shoulders only come up to my belly button, which means I can actually look down and see the top of his head. He is wearing the whitest sneakers I've ever seen in my life, and he's holding a square metal box with flowers painted on it.

"What's in the box?" Dillon asks him.

"Cookies," he says. "For Mrs. Beam."

I look at Ravi in his weird flat clothes, holding his flowery little box of cookies, and wonder if he realizes he's a zebra.

"Boys and girls, please take your seats," Mrs. Beam calls from the front of the classroom.

Ravi walks up to her and hands her the box.

"My mother has asked me to bring these to you," he says. "They're Indian cookies."

"How sweet! Indian cookies?"

Ravi nods.

"Homemade," he says.

When Ravi isn't looking, Dillon puts his finger down his throat and makes a gagging sound. Lucy

Mulligan giggles. Sometimes I wish they'd just run off together and get married and put us all out of our misery.

"Please tell your mother thank you for the cookies, RAH-vee," says Mrs. Beam. "I'll be sure to enjoy one tonight at home after dinner."

Ravi turns and starts walking back to his desk. He looks happy, but I notice he's staring at my feet. He probably thinks I'm going to try to trip him. I wonder if he thinks I'm the one who swiped his mechanical pencils too.

After she finishes taking the roll call, Mrs. Beam tells us to do silent reading until it's time to go to gym. I pull out my book and turn to the place where I left off reading last night. I've only got a few more chapters to go, and I want to know how the story turns out. Dillon asks if he can go get a drink of water ... and I can tell he's up to something. Sure enough, on the way back he tosses a folded-up piece of paper on my desk. I open it up and there's a drawing of a bunch of people. Almost everyone is wearing a T-shirt that says I'M WITH STUPID on it, and under that an arrow pointing to the left. There are only two exceptions. One is a really tall boy wearing giant shoes that look like boats.

I'm STUPID, it says on his shirt.

Next to him is a woman in a striped apron holding a dirty diaper with a bunch of flies buzzing around it.

Her shirt says, I'm STUPID'S MOMMY.

Another day off to another sucky start.

CHAPTER NINETEEN

RAVI

....

My day is getting better by the minute. First Mrs. Beam had liked the naan khatais, then she was impressed when she noticed how far I had read ahead in *Bud, Not Buddy*. Now it is time for gym class. I was Junior School Sports Captain at Vidya Mandir last year, even though I was only in fourth grade. If American gym is anything like PE in India, then my troubles will soon be over.

I look down at my clean white shoes. Das Sir, my PE teacher at Vidya Mandir, would be pleased. Every day before class, he lined us up and first checked our shoes.

"They must be pure white," he insisted.

Thanks to Amma and her polishing skills, mine were always as white as snow.

Das Sir would sit in the shade of his favorite neem tree and tell us to start with some drills: stretching exercises, jumping jacks, and one round of running. I always finished first, Pramod a close second, and Ramaswami, the poor sod, came dead last every time. He was slow not only in reading, but at everything else as well, including running. Das Sir had no patience for him. Ramaswami had such a big belly that when he tried to touch his toes, he would bend his knees and Das Sir would give him a whack with a neem twig. We all laughed our heads off when he howled. After the drills before we played cricket, Das Sir would send Ramaswami off with the girls to play throw ball or tennikoit or kho kho.

The gym teacher at Albert Einstein Elementary School is called Coach Victorine. He has a funny nose, and no mustache, but he dresses exactly like Mr. Das—white shirt and black tracksuit bottoms. I am looking forward to impressing him—and everyone else—with my skills.

Coach Victorine leads us out onto a large grass

field behind the school. He has a canvas bag containing several metal bats and some large yellow balls. I've never played American baseball, but I imagine it's a lot like cricket. I feel a bit nervous, but how hard can it be?

I expect we will begin with some drills and running, but instead Coach Victorine chooses Dillon and a girl named Jaslene to be captains and tells them to pick their teams.

"Do the girls play too?" I ask the boy standing next to me. He's the one who rides my bus, whose name is Tim or Jim.

"Yep," he says.

Playing against girls is going to be easy peasy!

Jaslene picks first. She chooses a girl called Amy.

I wave at Dillon to get his attention, then point to myself.

"I was first batsman at Vidya Mandir!" I call out. I want him to know I won't let him down if he picks me.

He chooses the boy named Robert instead. I was sure he would pick me first. But I remind myself that Dillon doesn't know anything about my athletic abilities or that I was a champion cricketer.

It's Jaslene's turn to pick again.

"I'll take you," she says.

At first I think she is pointing at the girl standing in front of me, but instead she has picked me. I can't believe I am going to play my first game of American baseball on a team made of *girls*. This is all Miss Frost's fault. If she hadn't made me go to the resource room yesterday, Dillon and I would have had lunch together. I would have told him about the gold cup I won last year for scoring two centuries in our final cricket game. He would have picked me first for his team today, and together we would have beaten the other team hollow.

Jaslene chooses a few other boys for her team as well, so at least I am not alone.

Dillon will be surprised when he sees how well I play. I predict he will regret not picking me first.

It's time to warm up, so I grab one of the bats and give it a good hard swing. Baseball bats are quite different from cricket bats, and I want to get a feel for it before the game begins. The next thing I know, Coach Victorine is screaming his head off at me.

What have I done now?

CHAPTER TWENTY

JOE

....

Coach Victorine reminds me of a penguin. He has a long nose, like a beak, and when he walks, he waddles.

"Line up, ladies and germs," he tells us.

I played Little League for one season when I was seven, but I wasn't any good at it. Even with my earplugs in, all that yelling was too much for me. Plus I'm pretty uncoordinated. As soon as the coach figured out I couldn't hit or throw or catch a ball, I spent the rest of the season sitting on the bench eating sunflower seeds. I didn't mind. I like sunflower seeds.

I don't like playing baseball, but I like to watch it on TV. My dad is a Phillies fan, but I'm into the Boston Red Sox. They're epic. In gym class, instead of baseball, we play slow-pitch softball. Dillon and Jaslene Arnado are the best hitters, but Amy Yamaguchi has got mad skills too. Emily Mooney isn't bad either—which is surprising, because she's white as a marshmallow and so skinny her arms look like toothpicks.

Jaslene picks first.

"I want Amy," she says.

Amy Yamaguchi runs over and starts hugging her.

"This is baseball, girls," squawks Coach Victorine. "Not a slumber party."

Ravi is pointing to himself, trying to get Dillon to pick him, but Jaslene picks Ravi instead. He is so shocked he looks like he's about to pass out. Jaslene probably chose him because she feels sorry for him. Girls do junk like that.

Dillon and Jaslene go back and forth picking teams until finally Henry Futterman and I are the only ones left. Henry is as uncoordinated as I am, plus he plays the violin, so his mom wrote a note to Coach Victorine saying Henry's not allowed to climb a rope or catch a ball or anything else that might hurt his fingers.

"I'll take Futzy," says Jaslene, pointing at Henry.

So I end up in the last place on earth I want to be. Dillon's not too happy about it either.

"If we lose because of you, you're gonna be sorry, Pud," he tells me.

We start tossing the ball around a little to warm up, and all of a sudden, Coach Victorine starts yelling at Ravi.

"No Rec Specs, no ball! No exceptions!"

"Excuse me?" says Ravi. "I don't understand."

"You can't wear your glasses when you play ball, kid. It's a lawsuit waiting to happen."

"In India, I always wore my glasses when we played cricket," Ravi says.

"Well, in case you haven't noticed, this is New Jersey, kid. You need to go to the eye doctor and get yourself a pair of Rec Specs—like those." He points at Henry, who's wearing a pair of prescription goggles instead of his regular glasses.

"Can you see without those things?" Coach Victorine asks Ravi.

"Not very well," he says, pushing his glasses up with his thumb.

"Take your pick, kid—sit on the bench or play without your glasses," says Coach. "Up to you."

Ravi takes off his glasses and puts them in his pocket.

"I'll play," he says.

OUR TEAM IS up first. We do okay for a while, but then when the bases are loaded, I strike out and Dillon gets ticked off.

"Way to blow it, Pud," he says, grabbing his glove off the bench and stomping off to the pitcher's mound.

Dillon Samreen does not like to lose.

Amy leads off for the other team and she gets a hit. Emily and Jaslene get hits too, so Ravi comes up with the bases loaded. He's squinting pretty hard as he steps up to the plate, and I notice he's holding his bat funny, down low like a golf club. He swings and misses twice, but on the third pitch, he brings his bat up, catches a piece of the ball, and sends it foul.

"Good cut!" shouts Coach Victorine. Jaslene and the rest of her team go nuts, jumping up and down and screaming for Ravi to do it again.

Even from far away, I can tell Dillon is up to something. When he turns his head to the side, I see the gleam in his eyes. In slow-pitch, the ball is supposed to come at the batter in a nice high arc, but Dillon winds up and pitches a fastball right at Ravi's head.

"Duck!" I yell.

But it's too late.

CHAPTER TWENTY-ONE

RAVI

....

Coach Victorine comes rushing over to help me.

"Get the first-aid kit!" he yells.

Everyone crowds around. I check myself, but nothing is broken. There is no blood, just a painful spot on my shoulder where the ball struck me. A terrible thought suddenly occurs to me. My glasses! But when I reach into my pocket and pull them out, I'm relieved to see they are not broken either.

"What happened out there, Samreen?" asks Coach Victorine. "You forget what game we're playing?"

"Sorry, Coach," Dillon says. "The ball must have

been wet or something. It just got away from me. I didn't mean to hit him. Honest."

"It's nothing," I say, standing up and brushing myself off. "Please can I bat again?"

But Coach Victorine won't allow it.

"How about you take our young friend here down to the nurse's office so she can look him over?" he tells Dillon. "We don't want to take any chances."

As Dillon and I walk to the nurse's office, it seems I do most of the talking. I have so much I want to say.

"Can you believe Mrs. Beam thinks I need special help?" I laugh. "Ridiculous! You saw my Vedic math. Does she think I'm like Ramaswami?"

"Who?" asks Dillon.

"He was a boy at my school in India who couldn't read. Does she think I'm like him? Or Big Foot? All he did when we were in the resource room yesterday was talk about candy and look at sports magazines. Ha!"

"Make sure to tell the nurse it was an accident," says Dillon. "I didn't hit you on purpose."

"No worries, man," I tell him. "Do you know Kapil Dev, the famous Indian cricketer? He came to Vidya Mandir as the chief guest at our sports day last year. My best friend, Pramod, and I had our pictures taken with him. When you come to my house, I'll show you. You can see all my trophies too, and Amma will make dosas for us. Our garden is quite big. Maybe I can teach you how to play cricket, and you can teach me how to hit a home run."

Dillon smiles at me and winks. "I can hardly wait," he says.

When we arrive at the nurse's office, Dillon reminds me once more to explain that he didn't hit me with the ball on purpose. Then he leaves and goes back to class.

The nurse gives me an ice pack for my shoulder and tells me to lie down on a cot and rest. I close my eyes for a while, and when I open them again, there's a girl in a green uniform standing in the doorway, holding my backpack and jacket. She's from my class, but I don't remember her name.

"Mrs. Beam told me to bring RAH-vee's stuff in case he has to go home early," she tells the nurse.

"I'm fine," I say, sitting up. "I don't need to go home."

The bell rings, and fifth graders start coming down the corridor towards the lunchroom. The girl in the green uniform puts my things on a chair and leaves.

"Please," I beg the nurse. "Can I go to lunch now?"

Nothing is going to prevent me from eating my lunch with Dillon Samreen.

"If you're sure you feel up to it," says the nurse. "Let me get you a fresh ice pack to take with you. It will help keep the swelling down."

The nurse takes so long preparing the ice pack that by the time I get to the lunchroom, Dillon has already bought his lunch and is sitting at the table in the corner by the window shooting straw papers with his friends.

I look at the menu board on the wall. Today they are serving something called chili. I see someone eating a bowl of soup filled with red beans and tomatoes. In India, we call this kind of soup rajma. It's more of a North Indian dish, but Amma makes it sometimes anyway, adding plenty of cumin seeds and black pepper to make it spicy. Rajma is served with rice, but American chili is served with some kind of yellow bread that looks like cake. I have my tiffin box with me, but I grab one of the plastic trays anyway and tuck it under my arm. I have a plan I'm certain will help me fit in.

Big Foot is sitting at the same table where I sat on my first day. I walk past him straight to Dillon's table. I recognize some of the other faces—Robert Princenthal and Keith Campbell, Tim/Jim, Tom Dinkins, and the redheaded boy called Jax.

"Excuse me, can you make some room for me please?" I ask Tom Dinkins, who is sitting next to Dillon.

Tom Dinkins looks at Dillon.

"You heard the man—move over, Dink," says Dillon. Then he laughs and snaps his head back to shake the hair out of his eyes, Bollywood-style. I wonder if Amma would ever let me grow my hair long like that.

Tom Dinkins moves over, and I sit down on the bench next to Dillon. I place the plastic tray in front of me, unbuckle the lid, open the top compartment of my tiffin box, and transfer the creamy white raita into one of the small square sections of my tray. I smile.

Finally, I am where I belong.

CHAPTER TWENTY-TWO

JOE

....

"It was an accident," Dillon tells Mrs. Beam when he comes back from dropping Ravi off at the nurse's office.

Yeah, right.

Celena Gervais, who's wearing her dorky Girl Scout uniform as usual, volunteers to pack up Ravi's stuff for him and take it down to the nurse's office. She accidentally drops Ravi's pencil case as she's trying to put it in his backpack, and the last of his three mechanical pencils goes rolling under the desk. Dillon sees it, and before Celena can bend down and pick it up, the pencil disappears down the front of his pants. She hunts around for it a little, but all she comes up with is a balled-up piece of paper. Crud! It's that stupid cartoon that Dillon drew. Why hadn't I thrown it in the wastebasket instead of dropping it on the floor? Before I can do anything about it, Celena tosses the crumpled-up cartoon into Ravi's backpack and zips it closed. Two seconds later, she's out the door and on her way down to the nurse's office.

At 11:30, the lunch bell rings. Wednesday is chili day. Einstein's chili isn't nearly as good as my mother's, but the corn bread is decent, especially if you put a lot of butter on it. Mom is standing near the door in her red-and-white-striped apron when I get to the cafeteria, but when she sees me, she looks the other way. I have to give her points for that.

Ravi is nowhere in sight. He might still be in the nurse's office, or maybe he went home. I get my lunch and head for the empty table near the trash cans, but Dillon steps in front of me.

"It's a good thing Coach decided to call the game," he says. "If we'd lost, you would have paid for it big-time."

"I know," I say. "You told me."

He grabs a piece of corn bread off my tray and stuffs it in his mouth. His eyes are pinned on me like two thumbtacks on a bulletin board.

What was it Mr. Barnes had said? *The world is full of Dillon Samreens.* I close my eyes and take a deep breath, trying to remember the rest.

"Wake up, Puddy Tat!" Dillon shouts in my ear.

I jump, and Dillon laughs, shaking the hair out of his eyes. I wonder how much time he spends in front of the mirror every day. In fourth grade, our desks had been right next to the windows, and I'd seen him checking out his reflection in the glass all the time. Once, Mr. Barnes and I caught him doing it at the same time, and we both had to try hard not to laugh. Thinking about that jump-starts my memory, and the rest of Mr. Barnes's advice comes flying back into my head.

"You have to find a way to keep him from getting to you," I whisper.

"What was that, Pud?" asks Dillon, grabbing another piece of corn bread off my tray.

I look at Dillon and try to imagine that, instead of a crocodile, he's a harmless little rodent like a mouse or a chipmunk. I never noticed it before, but his ears are actually kind of small and round and set high on the sides of his head. And with his cheeks stuffed full of corn bread, he *does* look like a chipmunk! All of a sudden, instead of feeling nervous, I start to laugh.

Dillon's eyes aren't sparkling anymore. They're cold and dark, like two lumps of coal. "You want to tell me what's so funny, Pud?" he says.

As he hitches up his saggy pants, I notice his boxers for the first time. Of all the things they could be decorated with today—polka dots or clover leaves, taxicabs or buffaloes—he's wearing boxers covered with peanuts. Peanuts! My grandma has a family of chipmunks who live under her porch, and she always puts a bowl of peanuts out for them. Dillon Samreen—the crocodile turned chipmunk—standing there in his peanut boxers with his cheeks full of corn bread pushes me right over the edge, and I totally lose it.

I haven't laughed this hard in a long time, and every time I think I'm done, I look at his little round ears and his peanut boxers, my stomach bunches up and it starts all over again. I'm laughing so hard I'm crying now. Dillon's an expert at dishing it out, but he hasn't spent much time on the receiving end. He is clearly not enjoying this. Kids are crowding around, laughing and shouting, and I don't even care that I don't have my earplugs in. This might be one of the all-time greatest moments of my life.

"I'm outta here," says Dillon.

Mr. Barnes was right! I found a way to keep Dillon from getting to me, and it actually worked! For one perfect second, I feel like I'm standing on top of the world . . . and then I hear the whistle blow.

"Break it up," my mom says, pushing her way through the crowd of kids. "What's going on here? Joey, are you okay?"

When Dillon hears her voice, he turns around. His eyes are sparkling again. "*Poor Joey,*" he says. "Here comes Mommy to save her little baby. Or maybe she needs to change his poopy diaper."

Dillon looks like his old self again. He grins at me, shakes the hair out of his eyes, and walks away.

So much for being on top of the world. I should have known it wouldn't last. Once a zebra, always a zebra.

I look at my mom and shake my head. She just doesn't get it.

"Don't be mad at me, Joey. I thought you were in

trouble," she says. "I'm your mother. What am I supposed to do—just stand there and watch?"

"No," I say. "You're not supposed to be here at all."

I'VE LOST MY appetite. I can't even remember the
last time that happened. My mom has to go break
up a food fight on the other side of the cafeteria, so
I put in my earplugs, carry my tray over to the table
by the trash cans, and sit down by myself.

A minute later, Ravi shows up, carrying his jacket
and his backpack. I guess he didn't go home after
all. I don't expect him to want to sit with me, but I
can't believe my eyes when he walks over to Dillon's
table and sits down right beside him. Maybe that
ball hit him harder than I thought, because I'm
pretty sure he's lost his mind.

CHAPTER TWENTY-THREE

RAVI

....

"How do you like Einstein so far, RAH-vee?" asks Dillon.

"Actually it's pronounced rah-VEE," I say. "Today has been my best day so far. I've been looking forward to eating lunch with you since day one."

"Did you hear that, Dink? He's been looking forward to eating lunch with me since day one. Isn't that nice?"

"If you say so," says Tom Dinkins.

"Is that your lunch?" asks Dillon, pointing to the raita on my tray.

I nod. "There's vegetable curry too," I say.

"Let me guess—did your mother make it?"

I nod again. "Amma is a very good cook," I say proudly. "Would you like to taste the curry?"

Dillon smiles at me and winks.

"You first," he says, handing me his spoon. "Have you ever tasted chili before?"

"In India, we call it rajma," I tell him. "And it's served with rice."

"Yeah, well, this is American chili," says Dillon, pushing his tray towards me. "Don't be shy. Take a nice big bite."

I dip the spoon in the chili and put it in my mouth. It tastes horrible! It's oily and sour, and there's something strange and sandy about the texture.

Dillon is watching me closely. Something about his eyes looks different—they're glowing.

"What's the matter? Don't you like the chili, RAH-vee?" he asks.

I shake my head. "It doesn't taste like rajma," I say, unable to swallow the horrible substance.

"Must be all the hamburger meat they put in it," he says, slapping me on the back.

I cough and spit the chili out on the table.

"What the heck!" says Jax, jumping up.

"I'm vegetarian!" I cry, grabbing the sleeve of my jacket and wiping my tongue with it. "I don't eat meat!"

For some reason, Dillon finds this funny. He starts laughing, and pretty soon all the boys around the table are laughing too. I don't think it's funny. Amma would cry if she knew. And Perimma? I don't even want to think about what she would say. Dillon had made me taste *beef*. How could he do that? Didn't he know from my surname that I am Hindu, and eating beef is a sin? My head is swimming.

"You should see your face right now," says Dillon. "It's hilarious! Almost as funny as it was right before I winged you with that ball."

Dillon screws up his face, squinting as he imitates the way I must have looked trying to play baseball without my glasses on.

I don't understand what's happening. Why is he being so mean? Pramod and I kidded with each other all the time, but never like this.

Dillon starts rubbing his nose and imitating the way I speak.

"*What you are about to witness is pure magic, a secret handed down from ancient times,*" he says, exaggerating my accent.

Is this how American friends treat one another? I don't know what to do. If I get up and leave, Dillon will think I'm a coward who can't take a joke. I decide it's best to sit quietly and wait for it to be over. I look at the lump of half-eaten chili sitting on the table. I can still taste it in my mouth. Maybe the buttermilk and Amma's curry will help to wash it away. I use my cloth napkin to wipe up the chili. I'll be sure to throw it away after lunch so Amma won't find any evidence of the chili. I'll also need to keep my shirt buttoned up, to hide the bruise on my shoulder. As I open the bottom compartment of my tiffin box, a familiar waft of mustard seeds and onion drifts into the air, and I feel relieved.

"Disgusting!" grunts Dillon. "What is that?"

I dip my spoon into the rice, scoop some up, and hold it out to him.

"It's vegetable curry with okra and chickpeas," I say. "Do you want to taste it?"

He looks at me weirdly.

"Dude, are you kidding?" he says and slaps the spoon out of my hand. "Do you think I want to stink like you, *Curryhead*?" he says. "You've been stinking up the place ever since you got here. I have to hold my nose whenever you walk by. We all do. Right?"

Tom Dinkins laughs. "You got that right, Dill," he says, waving his hand in front of his nose.

I can't believe my ears. Is this really what Dillon thinks of me? What they all think? That I *smell*? How is that even possible, when I take two showers a day—sometimes three? If I smell of anything, it should be sandalwood soap and coconut oil.

Dillon winks at me and grins. He doesn't look like a movie star anymore. His crooked teeth and beady eyes remind me of Shakti Kapoor, the most notorious villain in Bollywood. All this time I'd been assuming Dillon wanted to be my friend—but I couldn't have been more wrong.

"I bet his mother stinks of curry too!" shouts Dillon over the laughter. "Everybody in that neighborhood does."

My face burns and my legs are shaking like they are having a fit.

I want to:

1. *Punch Dillon Samreen in the nose.*
2. *Insult his mother.*
3. *Tell him he looks like Shakti Kapoor.*

But here is what I do instead:

1. *Push up my glasses and rub my nose.*
2. *Pick up my things.*
3. *Run away as fast as I can.*

Dillon doesn't bother to follow me. I can hear him laughing his head off and slapping his sides.

"Come back, Curryhead!" he shouts.

But I just run, like I am running for my life.

CHAPTER TWENTY-FOUR

JOE

I don't know exactly what happened. All I know is
that one minute Ravi is sitting at the table next to
Dillon, and the next minute he's running out of the
cafeteria so fast those white shoes of his are flying
like a blizzard in a snow globe.

"Come back, Curryhead!" Dillon shouts.

I could have told Ravi not to sit at that table.
And I could have told him that it was only a matter
of time before Dillon would come up with a mean
nickname for him too. Ravi thinks I'm dumb, and
I'm pretty sure he thinks I was the one who tripped

him, but I can't help it: I feel sorry for him. It's not easy being a zebra. In fact, it sucks.

CHAPTER TWENTY-FIVE

RAVI

So here I am, in the boy's bathroom. It's the only place I could think of to go. After I wash my face and rinse my mouth, I look in the mirror and don't even recognize my own face. No one has ever humiliated me like this before. I thought Dillon Samreen wanted to be my friend.

Luckily no one else is here—all three cubicles are empty. I hang my backpack and jacket on a hook, pull down one of the toilet seats, and sit down, clutching my tiffin box tightly to my chest.

Everything has changed. I am no longer the person I was before. I am Curryhead now. Curryhead who has no friends and can't speak English. Curryhead who smells bad and doesn't know how to do math or play baseball. At Vidya Mandir, I was like Dillon Samreen—a popular boy who everyone wanted to sit with in the lunchroom. Now I am sitting on a toilet in the boy's bathroom, hiding from a bully. I think about Ramaswami and how I teased him about his big belly, laughing when Mr. Das whipped him with the neem twig. Suddenly it dawns on me: I am the Ramaswami of Albert Einstein Elementary School. Curryhead, a loser and the butt of the joke.

It seems I am getting a taste of my own medicine.

THURSDAY:
MACARONI AND CHEESE

CHAPTER TWENTY-SIX

JOE

....

Mia is hogging the bed, so I sleep crooked and wake up with a crick in my neck. Sunshine is leaking in under the bottom of the window shade and hitting me smack in the face. That's weird. It's usually still dark when I get up. I roll over and look at the clock. It's 10:45.

"Holy smokes!" I shout, jumping out of bed.

I throw on some clothes, shove my homework in my backpack, and run downstairs without even tying my shoes first.

My parents are sitting at the kitchen table, drinking coffee.

"What's going on?" I ask my mom. "Why didn't you wake me up? And aren't you supposed to be at work?"

"Bertie from the kitchen crew offered to cover for me, and you're not going to school today," my mother says quietly.

"I'm not?"

"Are you going to say hello to your old man?" my dad asks.

I go over and give him a hug. I haven't seen him in over a week, and since he doesn't shave when he's on the road, his beard is pretty scratchy.

"Is it my imagination, or did you grow another foot while I was gone?" he asks.

"I don't know," I say. "Maybe. Does somebody want to tell me what's going on?"

"Have a seat, Joey," my mom tells me. "I'll get your breakfast."

Usually on school days, I eat a couple of bowls of cereal and a smoothie in the morning, but my mother has made huevos rancheros. She and my dad have already eaten, so she loads up a plate with fried eggs and corn tortillas covered in salsa, and sets it on the table in front of me.

"Sprinkle a little of this on top," she says, setting a small glass dish of chopped-up green stuff next to me, "It's cilantro—filled with vitamin K. Let me know if you want hot sauce too."

Huevos rancheros is one of my favorites, but for the second time this week, I've lost my appetite.

"Are we about to have a family meeting?" I ask.

My parents look at each other.

"Your mom and I do need to talk to you, Joe," my father says.

Sounds like a family meeting to me.

"What do we need to talk about?" I ask, even though I'm pretty sure I already know.

My father turns to my mother.

"What's the boy's name again?" he asks.

"Dillon," she says. "Dillon Samreen."

Here we go.

"What kind of name is Samreen?" my father asks.

"He's Indian," I say.

"What's his problem with you, Joe?"

I shrug.

"Have you ever tried sitting down with Dillon and telling him how you feel?" my mother asks.

"Come on, Gracie," my father says, shaking his head. "Don't you know you can't talk to people like that? It doesn't work."

"What are you suggesting, Kirk, that he punch the boy in the nose?" says my mother.

"It would serve him right. These people come over here expecting to have it all. They ought to show some respect."

"What people?" I ask.

"Immigrants," my father says. "They're visitors in this country; who do they think they are, pushing us around?"

"Dillon's not a visitor. He was born here," I say. "His dad's a doctor."

"You're missing the point, Joe," my father says. "The point is you have to man up and fight back."

"Lower your voice, Kirk," my mother says.

"There you go again, Grace. Stop babying him or he'll never learn to stand on his own two feet."

"I know how to stand on my own two feet," I say. "I do it every day. You just don't know about it. You wouldn't even know who Dillon Samreen was if Mom hadn't taken the job at Einstein."

"We've been over this already," she says. "I didn't have a choice; I needed the work."

"You promised me you'd stay out of my business, Mom. *You crossed your heart and promised.*"

Mia whimpers. She can't stand it when I get upset. I reach down and pat her head.

"Your well-being is my business too," my mother says.

Great, now she's crying.

"How long has this Samreen boy been bothering you?" my father asks.

I shrug.

"Why didn't you say anything about it?" asks my mother.

"I can handle it," I say.

"I'm going to call and speak to your principal right now," my father says, reaching for the phone. "If you're not going to stand up to that bully yourself, I'll do it for you."

"No!" I shout, banging my fists on the table. "No! No! No! You want me to talk about my feelings? You want me to stand up for myself? Fine. Here goes—I *hate* that Mom works at my school now. I *hate* that she keeps breaking her promises and butting into my business. I *hate* that she has to wear that stupid apron and blow that stupid whistle in front of everybody. I *hate* that you're never home anymore, Dad. I *hate* that you think it's okay to call up my principal without even asking me how I feel about it first. I *hate* that you're always telling me to 'man up' and that you don't like people who aren't like you."

"Indians, you mean?" he asks.

"No, Dad—I mean me."

"What are you talking about?" he says. "You think I don't like you?"

"Why don't you ever turn down the TV when Mom asks you to?"

"Now wait a second," my dad says, "I'm not the bad guy here. I'm only trying to—"

"Let him finish, Kirk," my mom says, reaching over and putting her hand on his arm.

It feels kind of like I'm throwing up. I can't control what's coming out, and it's not going to stop until I'm empty.

"I hate that kids think I'm dumb and that teachers don't like me. I hate being afraid to raise my hand even when I know the answer. I hate that I'm taller than everyone else in my class, including my teacher, and that the only real friend I have is a dog. Most of all I hate Dillon Samreen, because he never, ever lets me forget who I am. *That's* how I feel. Are you happy now?" I ask. Then I pick up my plate, scrape the eggs into the trash, and go upstairs to my room.

CHAPTER TWENTY-SEVEN

RAVI

Perimma storms into my room waving a piece of paper.

"Wake up, Ravi, and explain this to me right now," she says, pulling the sheets off my face.

"What is it?" I ask, rubbing my eyes. "What's wrong?"

Her hands are shaking as she pushes the wrinkled paper under my nose.

"I found this in your schoolbag."

"What is it?" I ask, sitting up and reaching for my glasses.

"Look at me, Ravi," says Perimma, grabbing my chin and pulling my face towards her. "Tell me what's going on."

"What have I done?" I ask, trying to see what's written on the piece of paper.

Amma comes in, takes the paper, and sits beside me on the bed.

"It's some kind of drawing," she says, smoothing the paper on her knee.

I push up my glasses, rub my nose, and look at the paper. It's a cartoon of a bunch of people wearing the same T-shirt.

"Did you draw this?" asks Amma.

"No," I tell her. "I've never seen it before in my life."

Perimma snatches the paper from me and studies it.

"Who is this boy?" she asks suspiciously. "Is that supposed to be you? Has someone been calling you names?"

She's pointing to a boy wearing shoes that look like giant potatoes. I know who it is supposed to be.

"This isn't me. It's the boy who sits behind me in class. He goes for special help. I call him Big Foot, but his real name is Joe Sylvester," I say. "Whoever drew this cartoon probably meant to give it to him, and accidentally put it in my bag instead."

I hope this will satisfy my grandmother and put an end to the drama, but instead she starts up again.

"Why do you and Mr. Big Feet sit together?" she demands.

"Are you friends?" Amma asks.

"We don't sit *together*. I sit behind him. The seating is alphabetical," I explain. "*Suryanarayanan* comes before *Sylvester*. And no, Amma, we are not friends."

My mother knows me too well.

"What's going on, raja?" she asks softly. "You have to tell me."

I want to tell her everything. How Dillon Samreen called me Curryhead and how I ran away and hid in the bathroom. How I have not made a single friend at school and have been ridiculed and laughed at every single day since day one. I want to tell her that I have been tricked into tasting beef too, but I can't.

"What's wrong?" Amma asks, squeezing my shoulder.

"Ow!" I cry.

Amma gently pulls opens the top of my pajama shirt and gasps.

"What's happened?" she asks, gently touching my bruise with her fingertips.

"Nothing, Amma," I lie. "I just bumped myself."

Perimma turns on her heel and leaves the room only to return a minute later wearing her sweater and shawl. She also has a scarf, a red dupatta, covering her head.

"Where are you going so early in the morning?" Amma asks.

Perimma ignores her.

"Get up, Ravi," she commands.

"Why?" I ask.

"I am coming to school with you. I want to see for myself what's going on at this so-called Albert Einstein Elementary School."

"Nothing is going on, Perimma," I say. "And you cannot come with me to school."

"When did you start answering back to your elders?" she says, her eyes flashing. "It's all this American influence. Are you ashamed of your perimma now? Embarrassed of her saree and bindi?"

"I'm sure that's not how he feels," Amma says.

"What do you know about it, Roshni?" Perimma snaps. "Tell her, Ravi. It's true, isn't it? You wish your silly old perimma had stayed behind in Bangalore where she belongs, don't you? There's no place for me here in your new American life full of insulting cartoons and mysterious bruises."

"No, Perimma," I say. "I'm glad that you're here."

But she ignores me and goes on.

"I'll tell your perippa to bring the suitcases from the garage. We'll buy a ticket today and fly back to Bangalore."

Amma sighs. "Don't be silly, Meena Ma. Ravi just told you he doesn't want you to leave."

Perimma narrows her eyes at Amma. "You've poisoned his mind, Roshni. That's what it is. We both know you don't want me here any more than he does."

"Stop!" I shout. "The reason you can't come to school with me is because I am not going to school, Perimma."

"Are you feeling sick again, raja?" my mother asks, quickly putting her hand on my forehead to check for a fever.

"Let me feel your pulse," says Perimma, putting

her fingers on my wrist. Now all of a sudden her voice is quivering with concern.

"I'm not sick," I say, pushing their hands away. "I'm finished with Albert Einstein Elementary School forever. I quit."

CHAPTER TWENTY-EIGHT

JOE

"Joey?" My mom is knocking on my door.

"Go away," I say, pulling the pillow over my head.

But of course she ignores me. Why does she bother to knock if she's just going to come in anyway?

"You didn't eat your breakfast, so I made you a peanut butter and jelly sandwich," she says. She sets the plate on my nightstand along with a glass of milk.

"I'm not hungry," I say from under the pillow.

She doesn't say anything, but I can tell she's still standing there. I hear her sniffle, so I pull the pillow tighter around my head. I've heard enough crying for one day.

"I have to go to work," my mother tells me. "Your dad's downstairs if you need anything. I'll be back later."

After she leaves, I come out from under my pillow. I look at the sandwich, but I'm really not hungry. All I want to do is go back to sleep so I won't have to think about anything. Mia is staring at my peanut butter and jelly sandwich, whining. I pull off one of the crusts and toss it to her. She catches it in midair and gulps it down without even chewing. I would give her the rest, but I'm not sure if dogs are supposed to eat peanut butter and jelly.

I can't fall asleep, so I get up and play a couple of games of Brick Breaker on my computer, then I finish reading the last few chapters of *Bud, Not Buddy*. If the other books this Christopher Paul Curtis guy has written are as good as this one, I'm going to read them all. My appetite must be coming back, because I drink my milk and eat the rest of the peanut butter and jelly sandwich, and when I'm done, I'm still hungry. Thursday is macaroni and cheese day at Einstein. That's the only part of school I'm sorry to miss today. A little mac and cheese would really hit the spot right about now. My mom usually keeps a couple of boxes of the instant kind in the pantry, but if I go downstairs, I might have to hear round two of my dad's stand-on-your-own-two-feet lecture. Instead I decide to do a page of math problems so I won't fall behind. Right when I think I'm in good shape, I suddenly remember the "personal collection" assignment Mrs. Beam gave us. It's due tomorrow. Crud. Mrs. Beam had reminded us about it yesterday, and this time I'd managed to write it down, which is lucky because it turns out that it isn't a personal *collection* she wants—it's a personal *reflection*.

We're supposed to pick some object that represents who we think we are and then write something on an index card about why we chose the object. This is exactly the kind of touchy-feely stuff I can't stand. What am I supposed to do, bring in a pair of my earplugs and write *I have APD* on the card?

I hear a sound out in the hall, and when I turn around, I see a white envelope slide under my door. It has my name written on the front in capital letters. *JOE.* I'm not sure I even want to open it, but my curiosity wins out.

Dear Joe:

I'm not the best with words, but that doesn't mean I don't know how to say I'm sorry when I'm wrong. You said that boy Dillon never lets you forget who you are, but it's not his job to remind you—it's mine. You are smart and funny and the best son a father could ever have. There is more to you than meets the eye, Joseph James Sylvester, and don't you ever forget that.

Love,

Dad

P.S. Interleague Phillies/Sox series this weekend. Want to watch it with me?

I read it three times. It's the first letter my father has ever written to me, and it takes a while for the words to sink in. Mr. Barnes had a bunch of quotes on the wall in his classroom. One of them was *Writing can change the world.* I think I finally understand what it means. I also know what I am going to bring to school the next day for Mrs. Beam's assignment.

CHAPTER TWENTY-NINE

RAVI

I am sitting in the living room in my pajamas, drinking a cup of Ovaltine.

"Quitting is not an option," my father tells me.

"Your father is right," says Perimma. "Look how hard he is working in America, Ravi. Taking the train up and down every day, always on the phone. Do you see *him* giving up?"

Perippa picks up his newspaper and goes out to the living room to read in peace.

Perimma gets the bottle of red ayurvedic oil from the medicine cabinet, and Amma rubs some on my shoulder to relieve the pain.

"Put this on," she says, handing me the red sweater and matching monkey cap that my other grandmother knitted for me as a parting gift. "You need to cover up if you're coming down with a cold. Get back into bed and rest. When you wake up, I'll make you some rasam and rice."

"I repeat," says Appa as he straightens the knot in his necktie, "quitting is not an option."

My life is a mess. Sleep is the only escape I can think of, so I do as my mother has told me. I put on the sweater and the tight monkey cap, which covers not only my head but most of my face, and go back up to my room.

I wake up at 1:30 in the afternoon, dripping with sweat. I pull off the sweater and monkey cap and throw them on the floor. My shoulder feels a little better, but my sleep has not been a restful one. Miss Frost's face haunted me in my dreams.

Assumptions are often wrong, she kept saying again and again.

"Where's the monkey cap?" Perimma asks when I come downstairs. "The wind in this country will be the end of all of us."

"There's no wind inside the house, Perimma, and the monkey cap is soaking wet."

Amma must have turned the temperature up. It feels like an oven.

"Are you hungry, Ravi?"

"Hurry and eat your mother's runny rasam," Perimma tells me. "Then we will get to work."

"Work on what, Perimma?"

"Your mother and I have gone through your backpack," she says. "You have been slipping up on your assignments, Ravi. No wonder you wanted to quit."

She hands me my agenda book and points to something I had written on the first day of school:

> *Personal reflection: Bring in an object that you feel represents who you are, along with a one-sentence explanation for why you chose this particular object. Please write your sentence on an index card and do not put your name on the card.*

"It's due tomorrow, Ravi," Amma says. "Why haven't I seen you working on it? Did you forget?"

"Don't worry," says Perimma. "While you were sleeping, your mother and I have taken care of it."

"What do you mean?" I ask.

"We went to Staples and bought all the supplies," Amma says. "And I bought you more mechanical pencils too, raja."

I was hoping she wouldn't notice the pencils were missing. I know they disappeared, but I have no idea where they went.

"You're too soft on him, Roshni," sniffs Perimma. "Losing all his pencils and the napkin from his tiffin box too? If his father had been so careless with his things, I would have made him pay to replace them."

Amma reaches out and takes my hand.

"Leave your rasam to cool and come see what we've done," she says.

The truth is, Mrs. Beam's assignment *had* totally slipped my mind. Personal reflection. At first I had thought it would be easy; I hadn't even given it a second thought. I knew who I was. But now after three days at Albert Einstein Elementary School, I am no longer the same person I used to be. I am Curryhead, a loser who can't speak English and has no friends.

Amma and Perimma lead me to Appa's office. Spread out on the desk are colored markers, a gold pen and a silver one, white liquid glue, glitter, glass gems, and all kinds of other shiny stuff. A piece of white chart paper lies in the middle, and at the top, in her neatest cursive, my mother has written—

Ravi, sharp and shining like the sun.

The letters are gold, the borders decorated with glitter and gems as elaborate as a Tanjore painting. Under this they have glued down photographs, each with a shining border of its own. Pictures of me receiving the award for winning the Math Olympiad. Me, standing on the podium with a gold medal for running. Me, holding my certificate for best outgoing student at Vidya Mandir. They have even taken one of my real medals and stuck it on the chart with Sellotape. I should feel on top of the world, seeing all these reminders of my success, but instead my stomach is churning so badly I think I am going to be sick.

"Do you like it, raja?" my grandmother asks, her eyes twinkling with pride.

"I'm sorry, Perimma," I say as my tears begin to flow. "I can't take this to school. You were right. All of Perippa's hard work at the tea plantation was for nothing. I am a complete failure in America."

She looks at me, and her face is soft.

"Don't cry, Ravi. Everything will be okay." Then she pats me on the back and quietly leaves the room.

"What is wrong, Ravi?" my mother asks. "You have to tell me."

This time I do.

When I have finished pouring out my heart to Amma, she puts her arms around me and wipes my tears with her pallu, the end of her saree.

"Don't worry, raja," Amma says softly.

I want to believe my mother, but nothing she has done so far has helped me. Not the naan khatais, not the kan drishti, not even her black tongue.

"Ravi?" Perimma is standing in the doorway with my grandfather. "Your perippa has something to tell you."

My grandfather is wearing a warm sweater and a monkey cap of his own. In his hand he holds a small tea strainer he has brought from the kitchen.

"Come, Ravi," he says. "I have an idea."

FRIDAY:
PIZZA

CHAPTER THIRTY

JOE

....

"Do you want a ride to school this morning?" Mom asks. She's dressed and already wearing her apron. There's a flash of lightning followed by a boom of thunder.

"Sure," I tell her, looking out the window at the dark sky. "I'll take a ride."

I tip my glass up and drink the last of the strawberry-banana smoothie she made me for breakfast. No huevos rancheros, just a smoothie and two bowls of Cheerios. Like normal.

Dad comes into the kitchen. There's a piece of

tissue stuck to his chin where he cut himself shaving.

"Did you tell him yet?" he asks my mother.

"Tell me what?" I ask nervously.

"I'm quitting my job," Mom says.

"You don't have to do that," I tell her, even though I hope it's true.

"It's a done deal," she says. "I already gave my notice. Today will be my last day."

"Don't we need the money?" I ask.

"I'll find something else," Mom says. "To be honest, I'm not crazy about the job anyway. When I suggested to the kitchen staff that maybe we could change up the menu a little, offer some healthier options like quinoa or tofu or something, they looked at me like I was crazy."

I laugh. I'm happy to eat tofu and quinoa, but I'm even happier to eat chicken fingers and hamburgers. If my mother really isn't going to be the lunch monitor anymore, that means lunch can go back to being my favorite subject at school. Woo-hoo! There's another flash of lightning.

"Guess we're going to need our raincoats," Mom says.

"Game one, seven o'clock tonight," Dad reminds me. "We're still on, right?"

"Are you kidding?" I say. "Big Papi is gonna bring it home for the Sox. You think I want to miss that?"

When I go upstairs to brush my teeth, I find Mia hiding under the bed. She's afraid of thunderstorms.

"Don't worry, Mimi," I tell her, reaching under the bed to give her head a pat.

"Joey!" my mother calls. "Hurry up. The roads are going to be slick, and I don't want to be late."

I give Mia one more pat, grab my backpack, and run downstairs.

"All set?" Mom asks, handing me my raincoat. She's got hers on already.

"One sec," I tell her. I go into the kitchen, open the cupboard, and take out a small glass bowl, like the one my mother had put the chopped cilantro in the day before.

"What's that for?" she asks as she watches me shove the bowl into my pocket.

"It's for an assignment," I tell her. "I promise I'll bring it back."

"What's the assignment?" she asks.

"I'll explain in the car."

When I tell my mom what I'm doing for my personal reflection project, she starts to cry. This time, for a change, it's the happy kind of crying.

"You are one terrific kid," she says. "Do you know that?"

Believe it or not, I feel like I kind of do. I'm in a pretty good mood by the time we get to school. It doesn't hurt that Friday is pizza day at Einstein. My favorite school lunch of all. As we turn in the driveway, out of nowhere, this dark red minivan comes speeding around the corner and almost cuts us off.

"Watch out!" my mother cries, honking the horn.

The driver of the minivan honks back and doesn't even slow down; she just zooms past all the cars waiting to drop kids off, then cuts in front of the line and parks sideways so nobody can get past. A dark-haired woman in a long blue dress jumps out holding the biggest umbrella I've ever seen in my life. It's really pouring now. As my mom and I run across the parking lot together, jumping over puddles, the woman in the blue dress hurries around to the other side of the minivan and opens the sliding back door. A minute later, a little kid in a funny-looking red hat gets out. He's so small, at first I think he's in first grade or something, but when he turns around and I see the way he pushes up his glasses with his thumb, I know right away who it is.

CHAPTER THIRTY-ONE

RAVI

As my mother and I walk towards the front door together under our big umbrella, I notice Big Foot crossing the street with a tall woman in a yellow coat. The wind blows her coat open, and I recognize the apron she's wearing. She's one of the workers in the lunchroom, a person they call the lunch monitor. Could this be Big Foot's mother? Suddenly I remember the cartoon Perimma had found in my backpack. *I'm Stupid's Mommy*. The person who drew the cartoon was insulting Big Foot's mother, just as he insulted mine.

"Are you listening?" asks Amma, pulling at the

chin of my monkey cap to straighten it. "I made curd rice for your lunch today."

"I know, Amma, you told me."

"Wait, let me finish. I made curd rice, but I checked the school menu; the option for today is pizza. It's vegetarian, so"—she unties a knot at the end of her pallu; inside are two paper notes and two twenty-five-cent coins—"I thought you might want to eat school lunch today, like the others."

I want to:

1. *Throw my arms around Amma and give her a big kiss.*
2. *Tell her she is the best mother in the world.*
3. *Show her the page in* Bud, Not Buddy *where Bud says he carries his Momma around inside him all the time.*

But here is what I do instead:

1. *Thank Amma for the lunch money.*
2. *Look around to make sure no one is watching.*
3. *Give her a quick hug.*

Amma, Perimma, and Perippa are waving to me as they drive away. I watch until the maroon Odyssey disappears over the hill and I can't see them anymore. Yesterday I was feeling like a complete failure, but today as I walk into Albert Einstein Elementary School, I feel like the luckiest boy in the world.

CHAPTER THIRTY-TWO

JOE

....

Dillon Samreen jumps out of a black Mercedes three cars down the line. It has one of those vanity license plates you have to pay extra for. It says: ENVY ME. Inside I can see his mother looking in the mirror on the back of the sun visor as she puts on her lipstick. My mom only wears lipstick when she's going out to a party. She looks better without it.

The wind is blowing, and it's really pouring now. Everybody is honking their horns because Ravi's mom's minivan is blocking traffic.

"Do you need your plugs?" my mother asks me.

I shake my head.

"I'm okay."

"Pop the trunk, Mom!" Dillon shouts, banging his fist on the roof of the black Mercedes. "*Mom!* Are you deaf? I said pop the trunk!"

The trunk finally opens, and Dillon leans in and pulls out a big cardboard box. He wraps his arms around it and walks away without bothering to close the trunk.

Mom and I look at each other, then I run over and close the trunk. Mrs. Samreen doesn't say anything— she just flips her visor back up and drives away.

"Have I already told you that I think you are one terrific kid?" my mom says a minute later as we walk through the front door.

She heads off to the cafeteria, and I start walking down the hall toward room 506. Ravi is walking in front of me. He has pulled off his weird red hat and is trying to comb his hair down flat with his fingers. It's not working too well. Dillon Samreen is standing by the door when we get there.

"Morning, ladies," he says, flashing one of his evil crocodile grins. "Welcome back."

We both ignore him. Ravi goes straight to his desk. I notice he's carrying a small package wrapped in the same kind of brown paper his math notebook was covered with. I put my hand in my pocket and feel the little glass dish. It had seemed like such a good idea when I told my mom about it in the car, but now I'm not so sure. What if nobody gets it?

"Before we begin, boys and girls," Mrs. Beam announces, "I'd like for you to place your personal reflection objects on your desks, and bring your explanation cards up here and put them in this basket."

There's no turning back now. I hang up my raincoat and carry the glass dish over to my desk. Then I dig around in my backpack until I find the plastic bag containing my object. I had picked it based on its perfect shape and color. After examining it carefully to make sure it hadn't cracked or chipped on the way to school, I put it in the dish and take the index card with my sentence written on it up to Mrs. Beam.

"I'm looking forward to seeing what you brought today, Joe," she says as I drop my card into the basket. Then she smiles at me.

I don't know why, but there is something about that smile that gives me hope. Maybe Mrs. Beam will like the idea I came up with for my object. Maybe she'll realize that I'm not really a pain in the neck who doesn't pay attention. Maybe she'll even write something nice about me on my report card at the end of the year the way Mr. Barnes did.

But apparently none of those maybes are supposed to happen, at least not to me, because when I get back to my seat, the little glass dish is empty.

CHAPTER THIRTY-THREE

RAVI

....

Dillon Samreen is standing near the door when I arrive at room 506. I ignore him and his crooked Shakti Kapoor teeth and take my seat.

"Place your personal reflection object on your desk, and bring your explanation cards up here and put them in this basket," Mrs. Beam tells us. Before I can unwrap my packet, I first need to wipe off my glasses, which have become clouded up from the weather. Amma gets upset with me if I use anything other than the special wiping cloth Dr. Batra gave me to clean my glasses, so I open my backpack and pull out the cloth. Just as

I am about to remove my glasses, Dillon Samreen reaches around me and snatches something off Big Foot's desk. He pops it into his mouth and quickly sits back down, but not before I have seen what it is he's taken.

CHAPTER THIRTY-FOUR

JOE

It's my own fault. I should have known better than to leave anything out on my desk when there's a known kleptomaniac sitting two feet away. So much for impressing Mrs. Beam with my great idea. All I have left is an empty dish, which is exactly what I feel like at the moment.

Ravi has left his package sitting unopened on his desk while he takes his card up and puts it in the basket. Lucky for him, Dillon is too busy unpacking his own box to notice. Mrs. Beam starts talking to Ravi about the Indian cookies his mom had made for her, but I get distracted when I see what Dillon

Samreen has brought. It's a big plastic yellow star with a picture of—what else?—Dillon's face glued to the center. Perfect. I watch as he rips open a package of AA batteries and loads a bunch of them into the back of the star. When he's finished, he sets it on his desk, pushes the ON button, and the whole thing lights up and starts playing "Ghetto Superstar." Lucy Mulligan and her little girlfriends come running over. Pretty soon they're all dancing around Dillon while he sings along to the music.

"Ghetto superstar, that is what you are
Comin' from afar, reachin' for the stars . . ."

His singing is bad, but the girls don't care. I notice his boxers are decorated with yellow stars, and the top three buttons of his shirt are undone. Gross. I'm not sure, but I think he might have glitter on his chest.

"Take your seats please, boys and girls, and we'll get started," Mrs. Beam tells us.

I am in big, big trouble.

CHAPTER THIRTY-FIVE

RAVI

"RAH-vee?" Mrs. Beam says as I drop my card into the basket. My heart is pounding. Have I done something wrong? Amma had offered to write my explanation on the card in her neat handwriting, but I had insisted on doing it myself. Can Mrs. Beam not read what I've written? After talking with Perippa last night, I had been so sure that this assignment would be a proud moment not just for me, but for my whole family. Now all my other failures come flooding back like a giant wave. My accent, my math, my English, my manners . . .

"It's nice to see you," says Mrs. Beam. "We missed you yesterday."

"You did?" I ask.

"Don't sound so surprised." She laughs. "I wanted to tell you how much I enjoyed the cookies your mother made. There's a spice in them I'm not familiar with. Do you know what it is?"

"I'm sorry," I say softly, bending my head down again. "It's cumin."

"Don't apologize," she says. "The cookies were delicious. It was all I could do to keep myself from eating the entire box. I was wondering—do you think your mother would be willing to share the recipe for the—what are they called again?"

"Naan khatais," I say.

"*Non cah-tize*," she says slowly.

Her pronunciation is perfect. I think about what Miss Frost had told me about stepping on toes, and about how assumptions are often wrong.

"Mrs. Beam," I say softly, my voice quivering a little, "my name is not RAH-vee. It's pronounced rah-VEE."

She looks at me and smiles. I never noticed before, but her eyes are the color of pistachios. "I'm glad you told me, rah-VEE. Was that better?" she asks.

I nod my head and smile back at her. "It means 'the sun,'" I say.

As I walk back to my seat, my heart feels lighter. It seems things are finally looking up for me in America. But my gratitude is interrupted when I see Big Foot sitting at his desk, staring into the empty bowl in front of him. He looks so sad and I am not selfish enough that I have forgotten about the insulting cartoon, or what I saw Dillon Samreen take from the little glass dish on Big Foot's desk. This is my chance to redeem myself for the unkind way I had treated Ramaswami at Vidya Mandir and for all the toes I have stepped on at Albert Einstein Elementary School as well—my chance to set things right. I reach into my desk and feel around with my fingers until I find what I'm looking for, then I put it in my pencil box for safekeeping until the moment is right.

CHAPTER THIRTY-SIX

JOE

....

"We're going to play a little guessing game," Mrs. Beam explains. "The goal is to match up the objects sitting on the desks with the sentences in the basket."

Great. I've only been at school for fifteen minutes and my day is already in the toilet. I look at the empty dish. No one is going to be able to match it with the sentence I wrote. Not in a million years.

Ravi is busy unwrapping his package. I am curious to see what's inside, so I lean to my left so I can watch him. The brown paper is held on with about a million pieces of Scotch tape. When he finally gets it off, there's another layer of newspaper underneath, and under *that* a layer of tinfoil and a lot more Scotch tape.

"Before we start," Mrs. Beam tells us, "I'd like you all to quietly make your way around the room, familiarizing yourself with the objects on each of the desks. I'll give you a few minutes to do that, and then we'll begin our game."

Miss Frost always says that the best place to start is at the beginning, so I go over to the first desk in the first row. Amy Yamaguchi brought a teddy bear—or at least I think that's what it is. It's a little hard to tell because it's gray and it doesn't have any stuffing left in it. Not only that, the face is completely worn off. Whatever it is, it's ancient and probably doesn't smell too good up close.

Some of the other girls brought in stuffed animals too, or girlie junk like charm bracelets and flavored ChapStick. A lot of the boys picked video games or sports stuff—including Tim O'Toole, whose personal reflection object is his own front tooth. Everybody knows the story—he knocked out his tooth last winter sliding into a goalpost during a hockey game. Even though there was blood gushing out of his mouth, he still managed to score the winning goal, which is how his picture ended up on the front page of the *Hamilton Herald* with a caption under it that said PLUCKY LOCAL KID JUST WON'T QUIT!

I am about to start walking down the next row of desks when I hear Lucy Mulligan scream.

Mrs. Beam goes running over to see what's wrong, and pretty soon there's a big crowd of kids standing around Ravi's desk. This is one of those times when being taller than everybody else comes in handy, because I can see right over their heads. Ravi has finally finished unwrapping his package. Sitting on the desk is a glass jar filled with cruddy-looking water—and swimming around in that cruddy-looking water are three long, slimy, black . . .

CHAPTER THIRTY-SEVEN

RAVI

....

"Leeches," I say as everyone leans closer to see what I have in my jar.

Yesterday Perippa and I took a walk together.

"Where are we going?" I asked him.

"You'll see," he said.

Ever since we moved to New Jersey, Perippa has been very quiet. He eats his meals without a word, then goes and sits on the sofa to chew his betel nuts and read his newspapers. But yesterday as we walked together, he had a lot to say.

"What's this I hear about you wanting to quit school?" he asked.

"Nobody likes me," I told him. "They think I smell bad."

"It doesn't matter what they think. Quitting is not an option."

"I know," I said. "Appa told me."

"That's because I told your father that same thing when he was a boy, and someday when you have children of your own, you'll tell them too. Quitting is not an option."

"You don't understand," I said. "Nobody does."

For a while, we walked in silence.

"Did you know that in India, tea has to be plucked by hand, Ravi?" my grandfather said finally. "Three leaves and a bud, right from the very top of the tea bush. The tea pluckers pick the tender shoots and drop them into baskets that hang from their heads. When I was a young man, my first job was to work at the tea plantation. I had to stand in the rain and guard the workers, protecting them from wild animals that might be lurking nearby."

"What kind of wild animals?" I asked, but my grandfather didn't answer. Instead he took me by the hand and led me through the tall grass to the edge of the pond Amma and Perimma were always warning me not to go near.

"What are we doing here?" I asked.

Again, my grandfather didn't answer. He bent his knees and crouched down, careful not to let his veshti touch the muddy ground. I crouched down beside him and watched as he dipped the tea strainer in the water and began dragging it very slowly through the weeds at the edge of the pond. Two times he pulled the strainer out and we peered in only at dirt and dead leaves, but on the third try his efforts were met with success. Three long black wormlike creatures wriggled in the strainer.

"We used to call them Draculas in disguise," Perippa told me. "The tea plantations were infested with them during the monsoon season—they were much larger than these skinny fellows, but these will have to do."

"Do for what?" I asked.

"Perimma told me about your assignment."

"The assignment is to find something that represents who I am," I told my grandfather. "Do you think I'm a leech?"

Perippa laughed and pulled a small glass jar from his pocket. "Fill this to the top with water," he said, handing it to me.

When I had finished filling the jar, he dropped

the leeches in, closed the cap, and tightened it. "These leeches are a reminder of who we are, and where we've come from, Ravi, and of all the hardships we've endured to get here."

I thought about our house in Bangalore and my friends back at Vidya Mandir, especially Pramod. I thought about the way things used to be, the way I used to be.

"I don't know who I am anymore, Perippa," I told my grandfather.

"You are Ravi Suryanarayanan," my grandfather said, putting his arm around me and pulling me close. "And the Suryanarayanans never give up. We work hard, against all odds, and believe in ourselves. Who would have thought that I, a small tea plantation owner, would be able to send his son to a fine university and to help bring his whole family to live in America too? But that is what happened."

"I miss Bangalore," I said softly.

"Me too. But you will have many more opportunities here."

"It doesn't feel like home," I told him.

"Give it time," Perippa said, reaching for my hand. "Come, Ravi, Amma and Perimma are waiting. If we stay out any longer, they'll think we've been carried off by that terrible wind Perimma is always complaining about."

Everyone in room 506 is still crowded around my desk, trying to get a look at the leeches. The time is right, so I open my pencil box and take out the blue candy—the one Miss Frost gave me in the resource room two days ago. I put it in my desk and forgot all about it until this morning. Now this little blue candy is about to play the starring role in my big plan. I look around to make sure no one is watching, then I place the candy in the glass dish on Big Foot's desk.

CHAPTER THIRTY-EIGHT

JOE

....

I can't believe my eyes. I actually blink a couple of times to make sure I'm not seeing things. Is there really a blue peanut M&M sitting in the glass dish on my desk? The answer is yes, but what's weird is that it's not the same one I brought from home. I'm positive. That was a single; this is a double. Those are rare—especially the blue ones, which is how I know who put it there.

CHAPTER THIRTY-NINE

RAVI

....

"I'll get us started," says Mrs. Beam as she reaches into the basket. She pulls out a card and reads it aloud: *"On my honor, I will try: to serve God and my country, to help people at all times, and to live by the Girl Scout Law."*

"That's easy!" shouts Dillon, jumping out of his seat. "It's Celena. Who else would be dorky enough to still be a Girl Scout in fifth grade?"

Mrs. Beam's eyebrows are twitching.

"As I explained a moment ago, Mr. Samreen," she says, "the person who reads the sentence is the only one who's allowed to guess. In this case, that person would be me, not you."

Dillon sits back down, and Mrs. Beam walks over to Celena's desk. She is the girl in the green uniform who had brought my things to the nurse's office.

"Is it you, Celena?" Mrs. Beam asks, placing the card next to a loop of green cloth with medals and badges pinned to it.

Celena blushes and nods her head.

"Now it's your turn," says Mrs. Beam, holding the basket out to her.

Celena pulls out a card and reads: *"Blondes have more fun."*

"Gee, I wonder who that could be," Dillon says.

Celena walks over to Lucy Mulligan and places the card next to the silver hairbrush sitting on her desk. "Is it you?" she asks Lucy.

"Uh, duh," Dillon sneers. "Of course it's her. This game is a joke."

Mrs. Beam frowns at him, then holds out the basket to Lucy, who reaches in and pulls out the next card.

"I rule," she reads.

"I'll give you a hint," says Dillon. He turns on his ridiculous plastic star and the music starts blaring.

"Ghetto superstar, that is what you are . . ."

Dillon jumps up on his chair, sticks out his long tongue, and starts waving it to the music. The way it moves reminds me of the leeches wriggling in Perippa's tea strainer.

Mrs. Beam's eyebrows are not twitching any longer; they've become a straight line now. She walks over and turns off the music. "Please get down from your chair," she says.

As Dillon starts to climb down, he happens to glance over at Big Foot's desk. When he sees the blue candy in the bowl, his eyes grow very wide and a look of pure shock comes over his face.

Yes!

CHAPTER FORTY

JOE

....

"Do you know who the card belongs to?" Mrs. Beam asks Lucy.

Lucy nods, but doesn't move.

"Is something the matter, Lucy?" asks Mrs. Beam.

"I don't want to see the leeches," she whispers.

"What's so scary about a couple of stupid old worms?" sneers Dillon.

Ever since Mrs. Beam shut down his "superstar" routine, he's been acting kind of grumpy.

Lucy gives him a dirty look. Hallelujah! Maybe this means the wedding is off.

Ravi has his hand up.

"Yes, Ravi?" says Mrs. Beam. I notice she says his name right for the first time, with the accent on the second syllable.

"Could you please tell Lucy Mulligan that the lid on the jar is screwed on very tight? My grandfather and I made sure of that. The leeches will not escape. Nothing to worry about, see?" He lifts the jar and turns it upside down. No water leaks out, but turning the jar over like that gets the leeches all freaked out and they start wriggling around even more than before. I expect Lucy to start screaming again, but instead she walks over and tosses the card down on Dillon's desk without even looking at him, then she turns and smiles at Ravi.

"I didn't know you knew my name," she says, tilting her head to one side.

I look at Dillon to see what he's making of this disgustingly mushy moment, but he isn't paying any attention to Lucy. He's got his eyes glued to the jar of leeches.

I know that look. I've seen it a million times before.

CHAPTER FORTY-ONE

RAVI

....

"It's your turn to pick a card," says Mrs. Beam, holding the basket out to Dillon.

He groans. "This game is so lame. What's the point? You can't even win."

"Try to muster a bit more enthusiasm, will you please?" says Mrs. Beam. "Not every game has to be about winning."

If you ask me, Dillon is getting off easy. Mrs. Arun would have made him kneel down on the floor or sit facing the wall if he had talked back to her like that.

Dillon makes a big show of swirling his hand in

the basket to stir up the cards. His overacting is even worse than Shakti Kapoor's. I can't believe I ever wanted to be his friend.

"Abracadabra!" he says, pulling out a card and waving it in the air like he's done something special. Nobody responds—not even Lucy Mulligan, who is busy staring at me for some reason. Dillon shakes his hair out of his eyes and reads what is written on the card:

"Quitting is not an option."

He rolls his eyes. "Gee. I wonder who *this* could be?" Then he marches straight over to Tim or Jim—I still don't know which it is—and puts the card down on his desk. "Is it you?" Dillon asks in a voice that says he is confident his guess is correct.

"Nope," says Tim/Jim, shaking his head. "It's not me."

Dillon can't believe his ears. "What do you mean, it's not you?" he says. "It has to be you. Everybody knows you're the kid who just won't quit."

Tim/Jim looks at him and shrugs.

"It's not me," he says.

"You see?" Mrs. Beam's pistachio eyes are twinkling like little green stars. "Maybe this game isn't so easy after all."

"Well, if he didn't write it, who did?" asks Dillon, looking around the room.

I wink at him and smile.

"I did," I say.

CHAPTER FORTY-TWO

JOE

....

"He cheated!" shouts Dillon. "That's why I couldn't guess it. What do leeches have to do with quitting?"

"Would you like to come up to the front of the class and tell us how the two things are connected, Ravi?"

Personally, I would have been sweating bullets if Mrs. Beam made me stand up in front of everybody like that, but Ravi doesn't seem nervous at all. In fact, he looks happy. He pushes up his glasses and clears his throat like he's about to give a speech or something. I'm listening, but I'm also keeping my eye on Dillon in case he tries to mess with Ravi's leeches while he's busy giving his speech.

"Quitting is not an option," Ravi says. "This is what my father taught me and what his father taught him and what I will teach my own son someday too."

"Big deal," says Dillon. "What does that have to do with leeches anyway? I told you he cheated."

"Shh," says Mrs. Beam. "Go on, Ravi."

Ravi pushes up his glasses again. "I haven't prepared anything else to say. But I could tell you a story, if you like."

CHAPTER FORTY-THREE

RAVI

I rub my nose and push up my glasses. My hands are shaking a little, so I fold them together the way we were taught to do in elocution class at Vidya Mandir.

"For many generations, the Suryanarayanan family has worked with tea," I begin. "When my grandfather was a young man, he worked in the tea plantations. His job was to protect the tea pluckers from wild animals that might be lurking nearby."

I look around the room. Everyone is listening. Some are even leaning forward in their seats! I decide to bring a bit more drama into the story by adding a few details Perippa had not included in his version.

"Have you ever been attacked by a porcupine or a wild boar?" I ask, pawing the ground with my foot. "Have you ever seen a panther crouching in the grass ready to pounce, or been stuck in the middle of a war between two angry elephants?"

I pause and look around the room for dramatic effect. All those years of elocution lessons are really paying off.

"Imagine it is the monsoon season," I say. "Imagine the ground is still damp from the heavy rain—a perfect hiding place for the most dangerous creature of all. More dangerous than the porcupine or even the panther, this animal can latch on to you and bite through even the toughest flesh with its three hundred razor-sharp teeth."

"What the heck?" says Jax.

"Be quiet," Caleb Burell tells him. "I want to hear about the teeth."

This is no time to lose momentum, so I take a deep breath and dive back into the story.

"Well, my grandfather battled these tiny Draculas in disguise every single day. Imagine yourself plucking tea under a hot sun, when suddenly you realize you are surrounded by viscous black worms waiting to fix themselves to your body and drain your life-blood out. Look! There's one between your toes! Be careful! There's one behind your ear! Believe me when I tell you, these dreaded bloodsucking leeches can even crawl up your *nostril!*"

Just as my tale is building to its climax, I am interrupted by a loud choking sound. A moment later, the air is filled with a horrible smell.

"Check it out!" shouts Dillon Samreen. "Emily Mooney just blew chunks!"

CHAPTER FORTY-FOUR

JOE

Apparently all that stuff about giant bloodsucking leeches climbing up your nose got to Emily and she barfed up her breakfast.

Kids are running around screaming, Dillon is laughing, Emily is bawling, and Mrs. Beam is calling the office to tell them to send the custodian down to room 506 quick with a mop. I feel bad for Ravi. He was having such a good time up there telling his story, and now all anybody can think about is Emily's barf. Miss Frost was right: It must be really hard coming all the way from India to New Jersey. Especially when you have to deal with somebody calling you names and stealing your mechanical pencils—not to mention hitting you on purpose with a softball. I look at that beautiful blue double peanut M&M sitting in the bowl in front of me and . . . *woop, zoop, sloop* . . . all of a sudden I get this great idea.

CHAPTER FORTY-FIVE

RAVI

The smell of the vomit is overpowering. Girls are screaming, Emily Mooney is crying, and Dillon Samreen is laughing his head off.

Mrs. Beam tells me to return to my seat. Then she asks us to take out our copies of *Bud, Not Buddy*.

"We'll go the library and read until the custodian has had a chance to clean up. When we return, we can continue with our game."

"Poor Curryhead," says Dillon as I take my seat. "His speech was so bad the audience puked."

I ignore him and pull out my copy of *Bud, Not*

Buddy. That's when I notice a folded-up scrap of paper lying on the desk beside the jar of leeches.

I unfold it and read:

> *BEWARE! DO NOT TOUCH THE JAR!*
> *TRUST ME.*
> *JOE*

It has been a day full of surprises, and it seems there will be one more.

CHAPTER FORTY-SIX

JOE

....

As we line up and start down the hall toward the library, my stomach is in a knot. Can I really pull this off? Dillon Samreen is up ahead, sticking his tongue out at Lucy Mulligan while she ignores him. Ravi hasn't said anything to me, but I know he read the note—I saw him. I hope I'm right about Dillon, but the closer we get to the library, the more I wonder if I was crazy to think that my plan could work. And then it happens. The first domino falls.

"Oops, I forgot my book," Dillon tells Mrs. Beam. "I'll be right back."

Here goes, I think. *This is it.*

As I turn and watch Dillon walk down the hall, I think about all the mean things he's done—not just to me, but to Ravi. Zebras have to stick together. I want Ravi to feel the way I felt when I saw that double M&M sitting in the bowl. As I watch Dillon Samreen duck into room 506, all I can do is hope that after all these years I know him as well as I think I do. I cross my fingers and begin the final countdown.

"Ten, nine, eight, seven, six, five, four, three, two, one . . ."

"Noooooooooooo!"

The door bangs open, and Dillon comes flying out of room 506 like a bat out of you-know-where. There's a terrified look on his face and a big wet stain spreading across the front of his pants.

I can't believe it! It actually worked!

When I saw Dillon eyeballing those leeches earlier, I knew it was only a matter of time before he'd try to swipe them. And like everything else he's taken, I also knew where they would end up.

Dillon is jumping up and down now, swatting at the front of his pants until finally the glass jar falls out the bottom of one of his pant legs and rolls across the floor.

Talk about an epic sequence.

CHAPTER FORTY-SEVEN

RAVI

....

What kind of fool puts leeches in his pants? Loosening the lid had been a capital idea, nothing less than pure genius!

Dillon is running around like a headless chicken. Then the bully of Albert Einstein Elementary School drops his pants and runs screaming down the hall in his starry underwear. Brilliant! I say a secret prayer of thanks to my grandfather and to the poor innocent leeches who sacrificed their lives for this important occasion.

Later, after Dillon Samreen has called his mother to come pick him up, and the cleaner has finished wiping up Emily Mooney's vomit, we return to the classroom.

"Would you like to finish telling us your story, Ravi?" Mrs. Beam asks.

"No, thank you," I say.

I don't need to show off anymore. I'm not like Dillon Samreen and I never will be.

"I believe it's your turn to guess, Ravi," Mrs. Beam says, holding the basket out to me.

I close my eyes, make a wish, and pull out a card.

"*There is more to me than meets the eye,*" I read.

"Ahhh," says Mrs. Beam. "Now, that's a tough one. Especially for you, Ravi, because you're new here. Would you like to choose another card instead, something that might be a bit easier to guess?"

I shake my head. This is the card I wanted to get. The one I had wished for. I carry it over and set it down beside the glass dish with the blue candy in it.

"It's Joe," I say.

Joe nods, then lifts his head and looks up at me. I smile and he smiles back. His eyes are brown, the color of the cinnamon sticks Amma brought with her from Bangalore.

"How in the world did you ever guess?" asks Mrs. Beam, impressed.

"It was easy," I tell her. "These candies have four layers. Most people assume there are only three, but assumptions are often wrong. There is more to them than meets the eye."

"Did you learn that in India?" asks Mrs. Beam.

"No," I tell her. "I learned it here, from Joe."

CHAPTER FORTY-EIGHT

JOE

....

My mom and dad are both pretty smart people, but the truth is, they don't know everything. Turns out you don't have to punch someone in the nose or blab about your feelings to get your point across. Sometimes all you need is a little help from a friend.

There are some things about my life that are probably never going to change. Like for instance my awesome metabolism, or the fact that I have APD. But I've only been in fifth grade for five days and I've already noticed a big change. The other day when

Mr. Barnes told me that the world was full of Dillon Samreens, I was pretty bummed out, but now that I know it's possible for a couple of zebras to outsmart a crocodile, life is starting to look up. Not only that, but it's Friday—pizza day!

CHAPTER FORTY-NINE

RAVI

··

I have always been Amma and Appa's shining sun, and my grandparents' pride and joy, but today I have learned something important. Winning is not always about shining the brightest. Sometimes it's about sharing the light with someone who has been waiting in the shadows all along.

It is 11:30 and the bell has just rung. My first week at Albert Einstein Elementary School is almost over. Amma's black tongue was right after all: Things have turned out okay. As I pick up my tiffin box and walk out of room 506, I feel like a new person. I haven't decided yet whether I will eat my curd rice, or try the pizza today, but it doesn't matter because I know I will not be eating my lunch alone. When I get to the lunchroom, I know my new friend will be saving a seat for me.

And I am right.

ACKNOWLEDGMENTS

We would like to thank Lucy Calkins and our fellow writers from the Fall 2012 Teachers College Writing Workshop. Special thanks to Holly McGhee for being a fan of this book from the very beginning, and to David Levithan for his brilliant editing and clear vision. We are forever indebted to our husbands, Arun Varadarajan and Jim Fyfe, for their patience and support as we wended our way through this process, discovering not only our own voices, but each other's. Musicians John McLaughlin and L. Shankar, we are grateful to you for "Get Down and Sruti (1978)," which gave us a new way to think about collaboration. Finally, to our sons, Vaishnav, Vedav, Gabriel, and Nathaniel, we thank you for inspiring us and for blessing us with the most precious of all the connections we share—motherhood. This book has been a joy for us to write. We hope it will bring joy to those who read our words as well.

—Sarah and Gita

AFTER WORDS™

SARAH WEEKS AND GITA VARADARAJAN'S

Save Me a Seat

CONTENTS

About the Authors

Ravi's Glossary

Joe's Glossary

Fran Weeks's Recipe for Apple Crisp

Raji Suryanarayanan's Recipe for Naan Khatais

Saving Seats Together: Q&A with
Sarah Weeks and Gita Varadarajan

A Sneak Peek at *Soof*

About the Authors

Sarah Weeks is the author of over fifty books for young readers. Her titles include *Glamourpuss*, a picture book illustrated by David Small, and the novels *Pie* and *Honey*. Her award-winning novel *So B. It* was adapted as a motion picture, directed by Stephen Gyllenhaal and starring Alfre Woodard and Talitha Bateman. Sarah, a graduate of Hampshire College and NYU, is an adjunct professor in the prestigious MFA writing program at The New School in New York City. She has two grown sons and lives with her husband, Jim Fyfe, and their dog, Mia, in a little green-and-yellow house overlooking the Hudson River in Nyack, New York.

Gita Varadarajan was born and raised in India and moved to the US five years ago. She earned her master's degree in literacy education at Teachers College, Columbia University. Gita has worked with children all her life, in India, the United Arab Emirates, and now in the US, where she teaches second grade at Riverside Elementary School in Princeton, New Jersey. She is an adjunct professor of literacy at The College of New Jersey and continues to spearhead reading and writing workshops in India. She lives in West Windsor, New Jersey, with her husband, Arun, and their two teenage sons in a town house decorated with interesting objects collected from around the world.

Ravi's Glossary

amma (*ah-mah*) . . . . mother

appa (*ah-pah*) . . . . father

Arun (*ah-roon*) . . . . name meaning "radiance"

ayurvedic oil (*eye-yoor-VAY-dik*) . . . . . oil infused with herbs, valued for its natural healing properties

Bangalore (*BAHNG-ga-lore*) . . . . South Indian city, capital of the Indian state of Karnataka, officially known as Bengaluru

bindi . . . . (*bin-dee*) a dot worn on the forehead

Bollywood . . . . Hollywood of India

century . . . . a cricketing term for a score of 100 or more runs made by the batsman in a single innings

chai (*cheye*) . . . . spiced milk tea

cricket . . . . a British game similar to baseball

curd rice . . . . yogurt and rice mixed together, sometimes garnished with mustard seeds, coriander, and green chiles

curry . . . . combination of Indian spices and herbs

desi (*day-see*) . . . . Indian

dosa (*doh-sah*) . . . . South Indian rice and lentil crepe

dupatta (*DOO-pa-ta*) . . . . head scarf, usually
made of cotton or silk

ghee (*ghee*) . . . . clarified butter

iddlies (*ID-leeze*) . . . . rice and lentil steamed cakes

kan drishti (*KUN-drish-tee*) . . . . evil eye

kho kho (*co co*) . . . . Indian game similar to
American tag

monkey cap . . . . woolen knit cap partially covering
the face—similar to balaclava

naan khatai (*NON-cuh-tie*) . . . . an Indian cookie

Ovaltine (*oval-teen*) . . . . malted milk powder

pallu (*pah-loo*) . . . . end of the saree that drapes
over the shoulder

Pramod (*pruh-MODE*) . . . . boy's name
meaning "joyful"

raja (*rah-jah*) . . . . a term of endearment
meaning "king"

Ramaswami (*RAH-mah-swamy*) . . . . boy's name from
the Hindu god Rama

rasam (*RAH-sum*) . . . . spicy lentil soup

Ravi (*rah-VEE*) . . . . boy's name meaning "the sun"

Roshni (*ROH-shnee*) . . . . woman's name meaning "ray of light"

saree (*SAH-ree*) . . . . traditional Indian dress, consisting of a long piece of cloth, elaborately wrapped around the waist and passed over the shoulder

Sellotape. . . . . Scotch tape

Shakti Kapoor (*Shock-tee Kah-POOR*) . . . . Bollywood actor best known for playing villains

Suryanarayanan (*Soo-ree-yah-neh-RI-nan*) . . . . Hindu god of the sun

Tanjore painting (*tan-joor*) . . . . . elaborate traditional South Indian art form using gold leaf and semiprecious stones

tennikoit (*tenny-quoit*) . . . . game played with a rubber ring

tiffin (*TIF-fin*) . . . . a light meal or snack

tiffin box . . . . stainless steel box used to carry a school lunch or snack; several boxes can be stacked together; connected with metal buckles

tracksuit pants . . . . sweatpants

uppuma (*OOP-uh-mah*) . . . . South Indian breakfast dish

veshti (*vesh-tee*). . . . . traditional Indian men's garment wrapped around the waist and the legs and knotted at the waist; resembles a long skirt

Vidya Mandir (*Vid-yah Man-dur*) . . . . . temple of knowledge

Joe's Glossary

barf . . . . slang for vomit

baseball . . . . an American game similar to cricket

blab . . . . to talk a lot

blow chunks . . . . slang for vomit

Bon Appétit (*bone app-uh-TEE*) . . . . American cooking magazine

bow tie (*boh tie*) . . . . man's necktie that ties in a bow

boxers . . . . underwear that resembles loose shorts

Brick Breaker . . . . computer game

ChapStick . . . . popular American brand of lip balm

cilantro (*sill-AHN-troh*) . . . . coriander leaves

crud (*cruhd*) . . . . expression of disappointment

Girl Scout . . . . similar to the Girl Guides in India

Hacky Sack . . . . a small fabric or leather bag filled with pebbles or beads used to play a game with your feet

holy smokes . . . . American expression meaning "WOW!"

huevos rancheros (*hway-voze ran-chair-oze*) . . . .
Mexican breakfast dish

index card . . . . lined card used for taking notes

interleague . . . a baseball game between one team from the
American League and one team from the National League

jelly . . . . jam

Kohl's (*coals*) . . . popular American discount clothing store

M&M . . . . .candy-covered chocolate sometimes
with a peanut inside

meat loaf. . . . . combination of ground
meats and vegetables baked in the form of a loaf

mechanical pencil . . . . a pencil with a thin
replaceable lead that can be extended and retracted

oatmeal cookies . . . . chewy cookies made with
oats and sometimes raisins

Phillies (*FILL-eeze*) . . . . baseball team from
Philadelphia

polo shirt . . . . short-sleeve knit shirt with
collar and three buttons

puke (*pyook*) . . . . slang for vomit

quinoa (*KEEN-wah*). . . . . edible grain high in protein

Red Sox. .baseball team from Boston

salsa (*sahl-sa*) . . . . a spicy Mexican sauce made with tomatoes

shrimpy . . . . abnormally small

snow globe . . . . a transparent sphere made of glass or plastic, enclosing a miniaturized scene of some sort

Sports Illustrated. . . . popular American sports magazine

Staples . . . . American chain store that sells stationery and office supplies

tofu (*TOE-foo*) . . . . also known as bean curd, made from soy milk

tortilla (*tore-TEE-yah*) . . . . Mexican flatbread

trunk. . . . . storage area at the rear of a vehicle, in India known as a dickey or boot

Fran Weeks's Recipe for Apple Crisp

FILLING:

5 apples, peeled, cored, and sliced

½ cup sugar

1 tsp cinnamon

¼ tsp nutmeg

¼ tsp ground cloves

TOPPING:

1 stick margarine or butter, softened

8 tbsp sugar

8 tbsp all-purpose flour

★ For the filling: In a large bowl, combine apples, sugar, and spices. Toss with a spoon until apples are evenly coated.

★ For the topping: In a separate bowl, use fingers to combine butter and dry ingredients. Topping should be crumbly. If consistency is too sticky, add equal amounts of flour and sugar, one tablespoon at a time, until mixture crumbles into pea-size bits.

★ Butter a baking dish (a large Pyrex dish is ideal) and fill with apples. Cover evenly with topping mixture and press down.

★ Bake uncovered at 350 degrees Fahrenheit for one hour or until top is nicely browned.

★ Enjoy with a scoop of vanilla ice cream.

Raji Suryanarayanan's Recipe for Naan Khatais

2 ½ cups all-purpose flour
¾ tsp baking powder
2 sticks butter
1 ½ tbsp sugar
1 tsp salt
¾ tsp cumin seeds
½ tsp cumin powder (optional)
2 to 2½ tbsp plain whole milk yogurt

★ Sift the flour and baking powder.

★ Cream the butter and sugar. Mix in the salt, cumin seeds, and cumin powder (if you like the flavor of cumin, adding the powder is recommended).

★ Add the sifted flour to the creamed mixture. Knead into a dough, adding the yogurt as you do so.

★ Roll the dough ⅛-inch thick. Cut into round shapes with cookie cutter.

★ Place on a greased cookie tray and bake in a preheated oven at 350 degrees Fahrenheit for about 20 minutes. Remove from the oven and leave on a rack to cool.

★ Enjoy the naan khatais with a cup of hot Indian chai.

Saving Seats Together: Q&A with Sarah Weeks and Gita Varadarajan

To celebrate this Scholastic Gold edition of Save Me a Seat, *Sarah Weeks and Gita Varadarajan talk to their editor, David Levithan, about collaboration, culture, and chocolate.*

DL: *What were you like when you were Joe and Ravi's age?*

SW: When I was in fifth grade I was tall and skinny and wore glasses. I was also pretty funny, or at least I thought so! I loved to write stories, poetry, and plays, which I sometimes talked my classmates into acting out with me. My teacher's name was Miss Volmer, and I thought she was the most beautiful woman in the whole world. My favorite part of each day was when she would read to us out loud.

GV: In fifth grade I was shy and very quiet. I had just one friend. I loved to chat and crack jokes but was not very outgoing. I had great handwriting and even won a handwriting competition with a new Pilot pen my grandfather had gifted me on my birthday. Later I lost that pen and felt like I had lost my good luck charm. I wore two long braids to school, neatly plaited with a dab of coconut oil. I loved listening to stories, especially those my grandfather narrated on Sunday afternoons.

DL: *What was your school like, compared to the one Joe and Ravi go to?*

GV: Well, I went to school in Chennai, India. My school was an all-girls school, Church Park, so while there were people like

Ravi and Joe in my school, they were all girls. Since it is very hot in Chennai, most of the classrooms opened up to outdoor courtyards. I brought lunch to school in a tiffin box just like Ravi and ate with my best friend under a huge umbrella tree. I mostly ate yogurt rice and pickle for lunch and afterward we played tag, hide and seek, or sometimes basketball or kho kho (an Indian tag game).

SW: The biggest difference between the school I went to when I was a kid and Albert Einstein Elementary was that my school, Pattengill Elementary, didn't have a cafeteria. Kids who took the bus to school would eat at their desks in their classrooms but I lived close enough to school that I could walk home at lunchtime. My mother would have lunch waiting for me—my favorite was toast with Cheese Whiz and dill pickles on it. Don't knock it 'til you try it! After lunch, I would practice the piano until it was time to walk back to school.

DL: *Were there any teachers who influenced you in elementary school?*

SW: My sixth-grade teacher, Mrs. West, was the first person who told me I should be a writer. Many years later I went back to visit her and she still had one of my poems in her desk drawer. I can't tell you how much that meant to me.

GV: Miss Soanes was my English teacher in seventh and eighth grade. She was my favorite teacher because she remembered my birthday even after I passed out of middle school; she sent me a bookmark on my birthday each year with a quote or an important message on it. Miss Soanes is still a teacher in the same school. She is evergreen and even looks the same. Miss Soanes was a great storyteller and influenced the way I tell stories.

DL: *Speaking of teachers . . . you two met in a class, didn't you?*

GV: I was studying education at Teachers College in the fall of 2012 when I was invited to be part of Sarah's writing class. It was a rare opportunity, as only a few students were selected for this class. So of course I was over the moon! It was my favorite class as we laughed a lot and worked really hard. It was here that I learned I could write. I ended up writing a book with my professor. What more could I have asked for? It was a magical experience.

SW: Gita charmed everyone in the class with her beautiful voice and charming accent—including me. I'm embarrassed to admit now that I never said her last name while she was my student because I was afraid I would mispronounce it. Once we started working together, I asked her to teach me how to say it properly. Var-ah-da-RAH-jan. Now I can say it perfectly—though she sometimes makes fun of my Midwestern accent, which is not as charming as hers!

DL: *How did you come up with the idea for* Save Me a Seat?

SW: Gita wrote a short story in my class about a boy who moves from India to New Jersey and what his first day in fifth grade was like. That was the jumping-off point for our book. I'll let her tell you more about what happened next . . .

GV: I had just moved to New Jersey from India a couple of years before, and I felt the need to write about that experience. Sarah loved the story I submitted for class, and called me after the semester was done. She said she would help me find a publisher OR write this story with me. I couldn't believe my ears. The rest, as they say, is history.

DL: *What was your writing process like?*

GV: In the beginning we wrote back and forth. I write long, and Sarah is a genius at paring it down and finding the "gold," as she says. So the story truly became ours, not just hers and mine. Each night I would write a chapter and send it off. I would wake up to find some suggestions and edits that would make the story so much richer. It was a true collaboration, one that was fluid and easy, one that capitalized on our strengths and most of all one that was based on respect for each other's voice.

SW: Gita likes to write late at night and I am a morning person. I would get up in the morning and run to my computer to see what she had sent, then I would spend the morning responding to it with ideas and suggestions for what might happen next. We also spent many hours talking on the phone. We liked to read our work out loud to each other—laughing and sometimes crying at the sad parts.

DL: *One of the great themes in the book is how we can learn from each other. Sarah, what was the most interesting thing you learned from working with Gita and reading about Ravi?*

SW: I learned SO many interesting things from Gita—not just about life in India, but also about collaboration. I had never written a book with another person. For me the writing process had always been a solitary one. Working with Gita taught me that having a partner to bounce your ideas off can inspire stories you never would have told on your own. Also, the process of writing a book together was much faster than writing on my own. I am SO excited to be writing another book with Gita now!

DL: *Gita, what was the most interesting thing you learned from working with Sarah and reading about Joe?*

GV: Sarah is a very hardworking writer. She works fast and is extremely focused. I really learned that writing involves timelines, organization, planning, and hard work. I think she provided the routine and discipline I needed as a first-time writer.

Apart from a strong work ethic, I learned so much about American culture from Sarah. While I am very open-minded, it was really enriching to develop a deep relationship with Sarah, as it helped me gain firsthand experience of what it means to be American. It helped me question the assumptions and stereotypes that many of my friends and family in India have about Americans.

DL: *Family plays such an important role in the story. What stories did you draw upon to create your characters' families?*

GV: My grandfather was a very patient man. Perippa too plays that role though in a very quiet way. My mother is a quiet person who always stands by me; so is Amma. Ravi was a star in India, but here in America he is struggling to fit in. While I am not like Ravi at all, in the way I look or act, this particular part of finding who I am in America is very similar to Ravi's experience. So yes, some of the characters in the story do mirror people in my life, including me.

SW: Joe and his family are not based on my family at all. Joe is an only child, while I had an older sister and brother growing up. His dad isn't very open-minded about people who are different from him, but my father was not like that at all. Although my characters are fictional, I always use elements of my life when I create my stories. For instance, like me, Joe's mom loves to cook and Joe's dog is based on my dog Mia. Also, Joe's love of the Red Sox comes from the fact that my two sons are both big fans. Go Sox!

DL: *Your love for Joe and Ravi shines from the page (even when they don't always do the right thing!). But I'm curious—Joe and Ravi aside, who was your favorite character to write?*

SW: I love Perrima! Hands down she was my favorite character to create and write dialogue for. Gita was shy at times about writing some of the horrible things that came out of Ravi's grandmother's mouth, but I had a blast thinking of insulting things for her to say, like when she accuses Americans of being beef-eating, divorced cowboys. Youch!

GV: I love Dillon. His resemblance to Shakti Kapoor (the greatest villain in Bollywood), his long wagging tongue, his kleptomania, his extra-mean streak, his popularity with the girls, and his absolute disdain for adults were so fun to explore and write about.

DL: *Another crucial character in the book is . . . an M&M. So I have to ask: Do you prefer peanut or plain M&Ms? And do you have a favorite M&M color?*

GV: Well I prefer the peanut M&Ms to the plain ones. It was Sarah who taught me how to discover the four layers in a peanut M&M. I don't mind any color, but now after *Save Me a Seat*, blue is definitely my favorite.

SW: I am a big fan of peanut M&Ms. I know for a fact that the colors all taste exactly the same, but I still have a favorite: blue. And blue doubles? Well, those are the BEST!

DL: *One of the amazing things about* Save Me a Seat *is that you have these two important main characters . . . and they don't speak to each other until the very, very end. What was it like to write a book where the main characters are in the same room, taking each other in, but not communicating with words? Why did you choose to do this?*

SW: To be honest, it was challenging to have two main characters in the story who never spoke to each other. There were times when I wondered if we had made a crazy decision to do that, but in the end, I feel like it added an important element to the story. One of the themes in our book is assumptions people make about each other. The fact that Ravi and Joe never speak made it easier for them to assume things that weren't true.

GV: I think it was really cool that the two main characters never spoke to each other. In fact, a lot of the assumptions we make about each other come from not taking the time or making the effort to get to know the other person. So this strategy really paid off in our story.

DL: Save Me a Seat *has had a remarkable life out in the world so far, and I know both of you have talked to readers about the book. Can you share one of your favorite reactions?*

GV: One of my favorite reactions was when an Indian girl in a crowd of white faces raised her hand and asked me, "Since you are Indian, do you know my mother Priya?" It was so endearing. She went on to also ask if I wore the bindi and saree, and when I said yes, she began shaking with joy. Later I was told she was new in school and *Save Me a Seat* helped her feel important and valued.

SW: I have received so many wonderful letters from kids who say things like, "Ravi's story feels like it is about me!" I can't imagine a higher compliment for an author to receive. I feel very fortunate to have learned so much about Indian culture from Gita. I never could have created this story without her.

DL: *If readers loved* Save Me a Seat, *can you recommend some other books they might like?*

SW: There are SO many wonderful books out there to choose from. Some of my favorite authors are Pam Muñoz Ryan, Richard Peck, and Cynthia Lord. Of my own books, I think fans of this book might enjoy *Cheese* and *Pie*. To read, that is, not eat!

GV: I think you will definitely like all of Sarah's books especially *Cheese*, *Pie*, and *As Simple as It Seems*. You might also enjoy *Wonder* by R. J. Palacio.

DL: *Thank you, Sarah and Gita!*

Turn the page for a glimpse
of Sarah Weeks's heart-
warming new novel, a sequel
to her classic *So B. It!*

CHAPTER ONE

More than a bird loves to sing

I saw a white rabbit with one bent ear hopping over a giant spoon filled with whipped cream. That's what it looked like to me anyway. I'd been lying on my back in the bed of my father's rusty old pickup truck all morning, watching clouds. I tapped the end of my nose once, twice, three times with my finger and wished I'd remembered to put on sunscreen.

"Aurora!" my mother called from the house. "Lunch!"

"Coming!" I called back, but I didn't move. I was busy watching the rabbit turn into a girl with a puffy white bow in her hair. Lindsey Toffle, a girl who sat in front of me at school, wore a bow like that sometimes. It was so big I had to lean over to one side in order to see the blackboard.

The cloud broke apart and drifted away, but I was still lying there thinking about Lindsey Toffle. She was the most popular girl in my class and she didn't like me at all. It might have had something to do with the fact that I bit her once when we were in kindergarten, but (A) that was a long time ago, and (B) it hardly even left a mark. The main reason Lindsey Toffle didn't like me was because I was weird.

Sometimes, just for fun, when I walked down the hall I would hop on one foot or flap my arms and pretend to be a bird. Other times, also for fun, I would speak in a British accent or a language I'd made up called Beepish. I wore my T-shirts inside out because the tags bothered me even after my mother cut them out. I liked counting stuff, I was obsessed with coloring in the middle of *o*'s, and I had an annoying habit of dividing my sentences into two parts, with an (A) and a (B).

"Aurora!" my mother called again.

"Coming!"

I climbed out of the back of the truck and dusted myself off. Duck was busy digging a hole in the corner of the yard, shooting dirt out from between his hind legs like a maniac. When I whistled through my teeth, he stopped digging and came running. Duck was the sweetest, smartest, most loyal dog in the world, and as if that wasn't reason enough to love him, the inside of his ears smelled like popcorn.

I pulled open the screen door. "After you, guv'nor," I said in my best Cockney accent. Duck followed me into the kitchen and flopped down expectantly on the floor beside my chair.

"Don't think I haven't noticed you two are in cahoots," my mother said, setting a bowl of tomato soup and half a grilled cheese sandwich in front of me. "If I had a nickel for every scrap of food you've 'accidentally' dropped on the floor for that dog, I'd be a wealthy woman."

My father says the reason my mother's name is Ruby is because her parents took one look at her and knew she was a gem. She likes it when he says that. I can tell because her eyes sparkle.

"How's the quilt coming along?" I asked, biting off a corner of my sandwich. I had a system—corners first, then a row of tiny, evenly spaced bites across the top edge to make it look like waves. I counted sixteen bites in all, including the corners.

The quilt was for Heidi, a girl who had stayed with my parents for a little while before I was born. She wasn't a girl anymore; she was all grown up now and married to a very tall man named Paul. The quilt was for the baby Heidi was expecting, a little girl due in July.

"I'm almost finished with the border," my mother told me. "I don't know if Heidi will recognize the fabric, but it's from the curtains that used to hang in that back bedroom before it was yours. That's where Heidi slept when she was here."

"I know," I said, tapping the edge of the table once, twice, three times. Tapping was another weird thing I liked to do—always in threes, because three was my favorite number.

I'd never met Heidi, but I'd heard a lot of stories about her. There was the one about the jar of jelly beans and the one about the penny getting stuck in the vacuum cleaner. There was the one about Heidi's mama learning how to use the electric can opener and the one about Bernadette, Heidi's neighbor, making a bet with my father that Heidi could guess ten coin flips in a row without missing. I'd heard the Heidi stories so many times I knew them all by heart, but my favorite by far was the one about me. My mother always told it the same way:

"We'd been waiting for a baby of our own for a very long time. We'd all but given up hope. Then one day, out of the blue, a stranger arrived in Liberty. Her name was Heidi It. From the outside she looked like an ordinary girl, but inside she had a powerful streak of luck running through her like a river. Heidi didn't stay for very long, but her visit changed our lives forever. Before she left she passed her good luck along to your father and me, and the following winter, on a snowy Monday morning, you were born."

That was it. The whole story. But the message came through loud and clear: My parents had been given a whole lot of luck, and they'd used it all up wishing for me.